OWLY

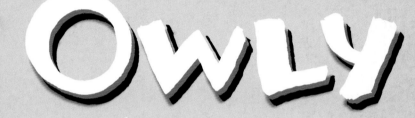

THE WAY HOME

OWLY

THE WAY HOME

ANDY RUNTON

graphix

An Imprint of

SCHOLASTIC

All rights reserved. Published by Graphix, an imprint of Scholastic
Inc., *Publishers since 1920.* SCHOLASTIC, GRAPHIX, and associated logos
are trademarks and/or registered trademarks of Scholastic Inc.

The publisher does not have any control over and does not assume
any responsibility for author or third-party websites or their content.

Library of Congress Control Number: 2019936368

ISBN 978-1-338-30066-6 (hardcover)
ISBN 978-1-338-30065-9 (paperback)

10 9 8 7 6 5 4 3 2 1   20 21 22 23 24

Printed in Malaysia 108
First edition, February 2020
Edited by Megan Peace
Book design by Phil Falco
Publisher: David Saylor

J
GRAPHIC
NOVEL
RUNTON
ANDY

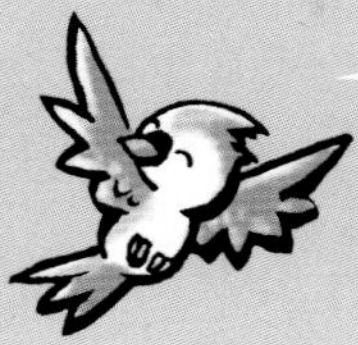

FOR MY MOM

WHO BROUGHT THE JOY
OF THE LITTLE BIRDS
INTO MY LIFE

CONTENTS

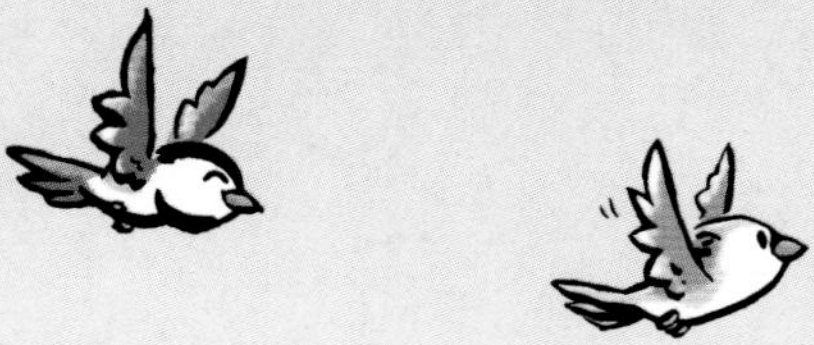

FINDING HOME

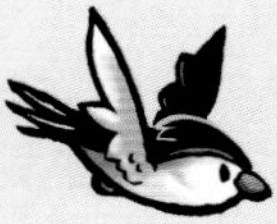

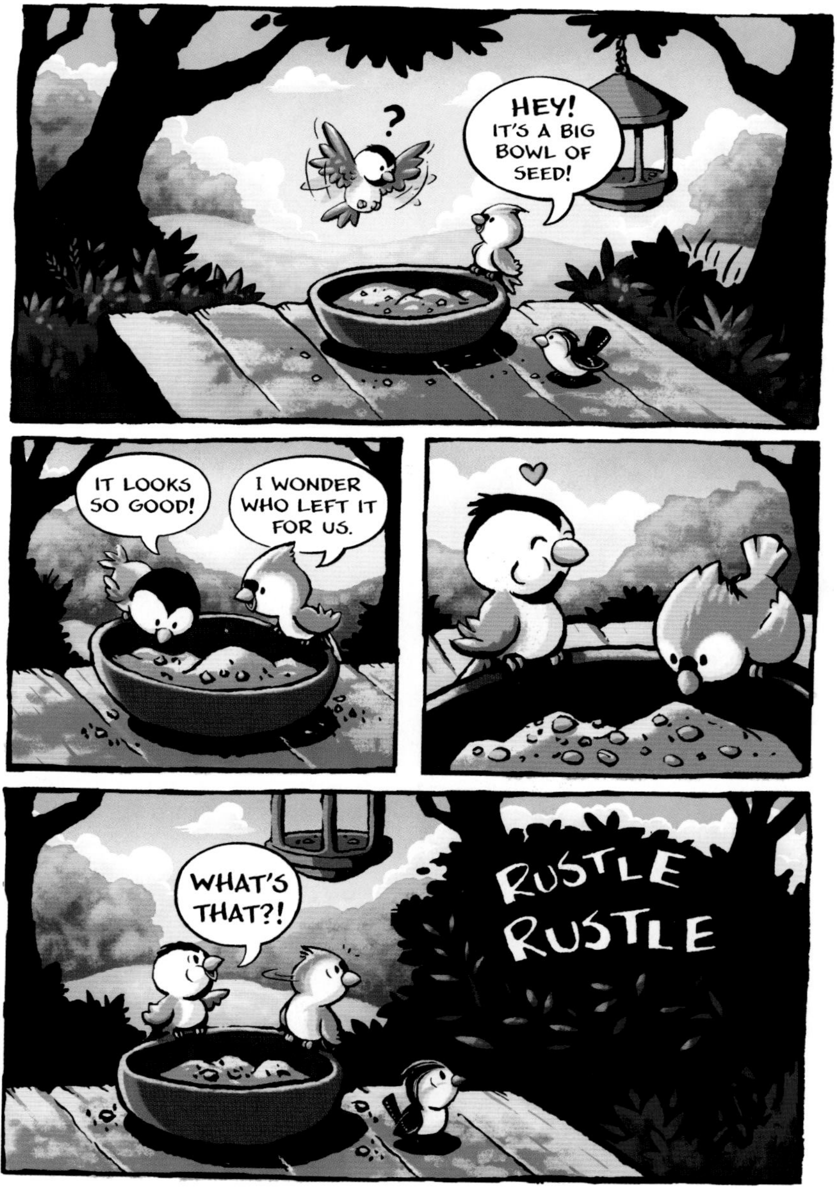
?
HEY! IT'S A BIG BOWL OF SEED!
IT LOOKS SO GOOD!
I WONDER WHO LEFT IT FOR US.
WHAT'S THAT?!
RUSTLE RUSTLE

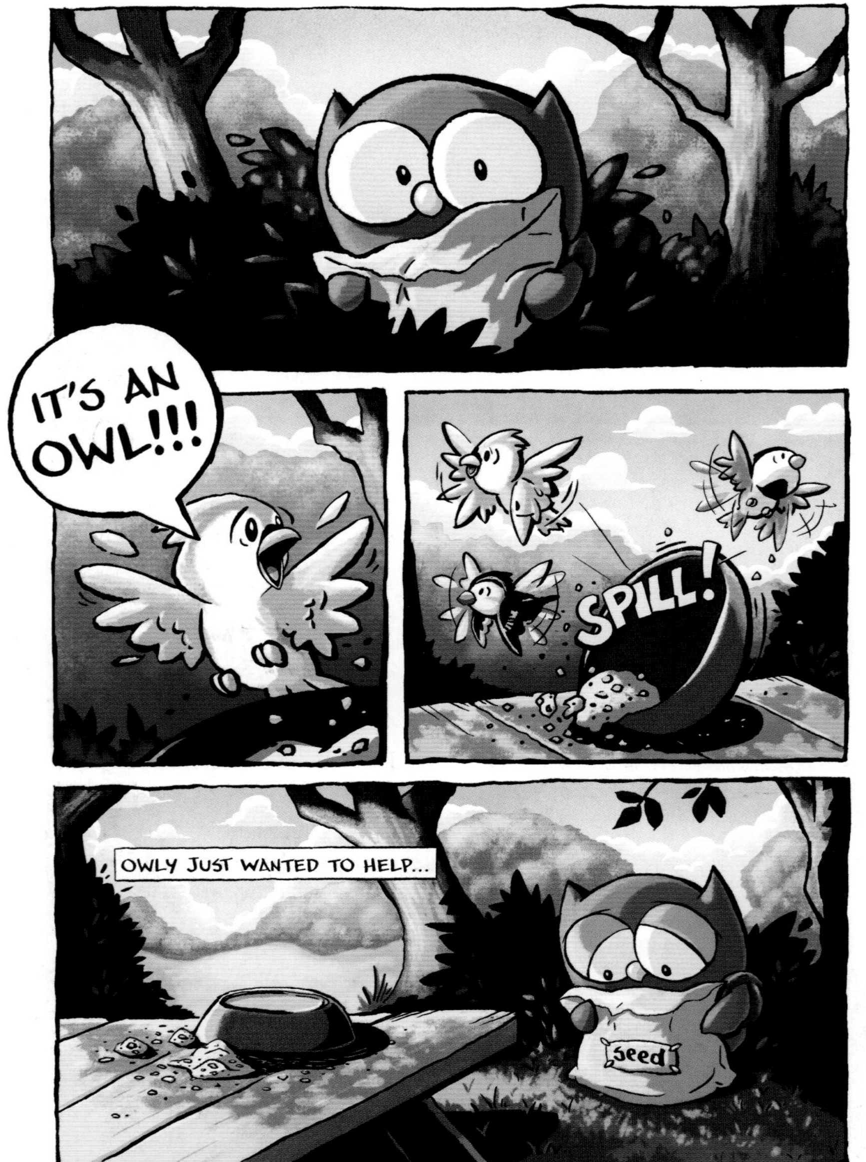
IT'S AN OWL!!!
SPILL!
OWLY JUST WANTED TO HELP...
seed

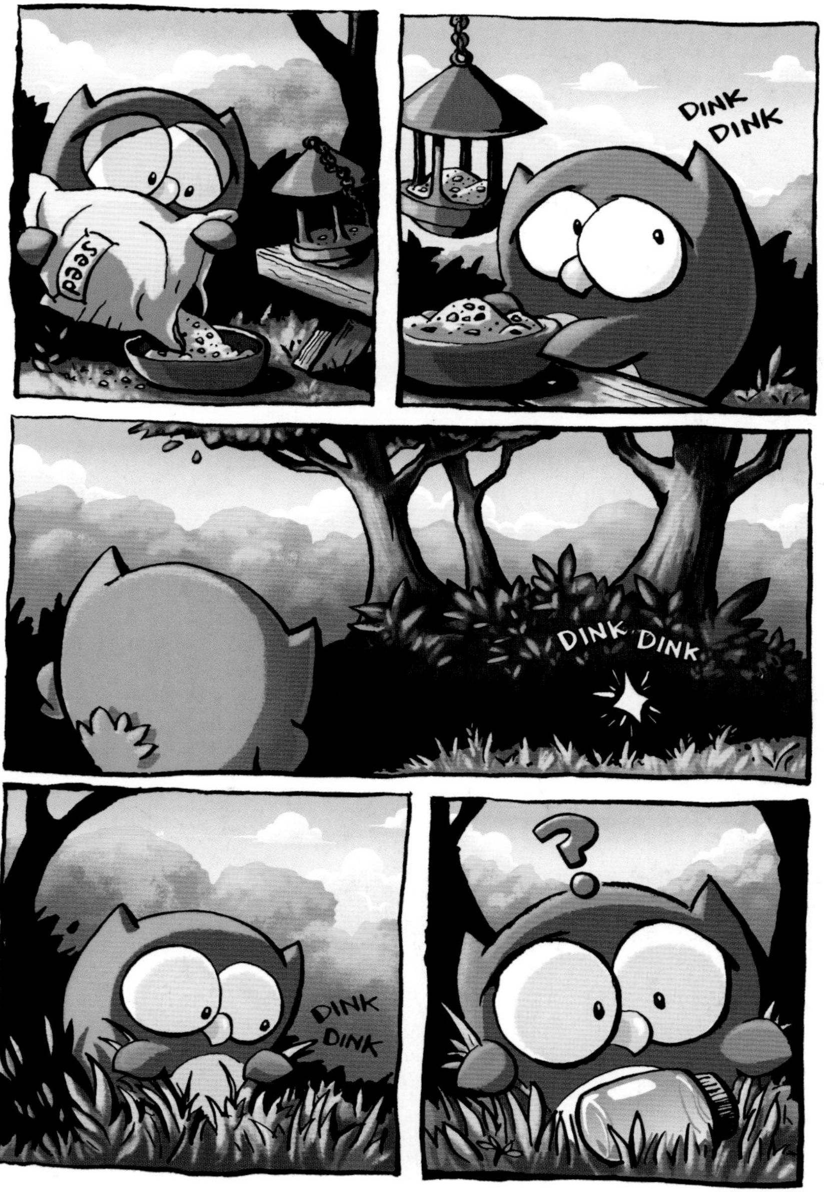
Seed
DINK
DINK
DINK DINK
DINK
DINK
?

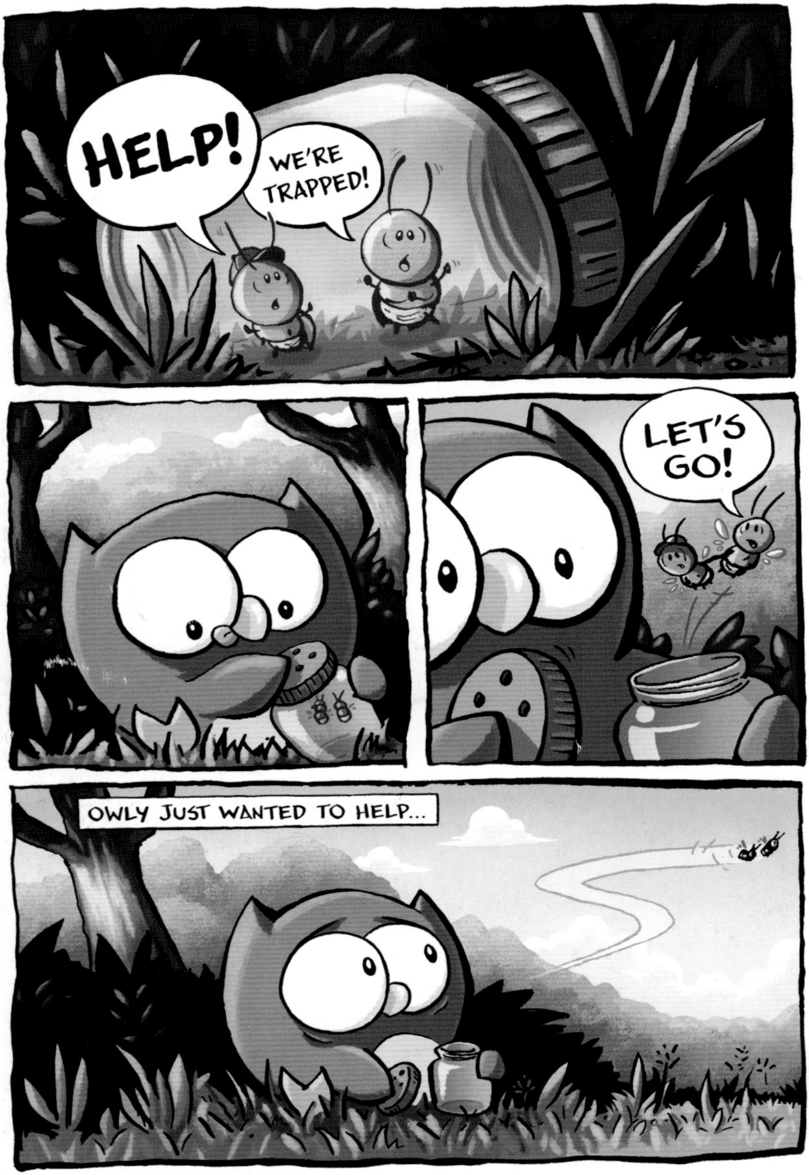
HELP!
WE'RE TRAPPED!
LET'S GO!
OWLY JUST WANTED TO HELP...

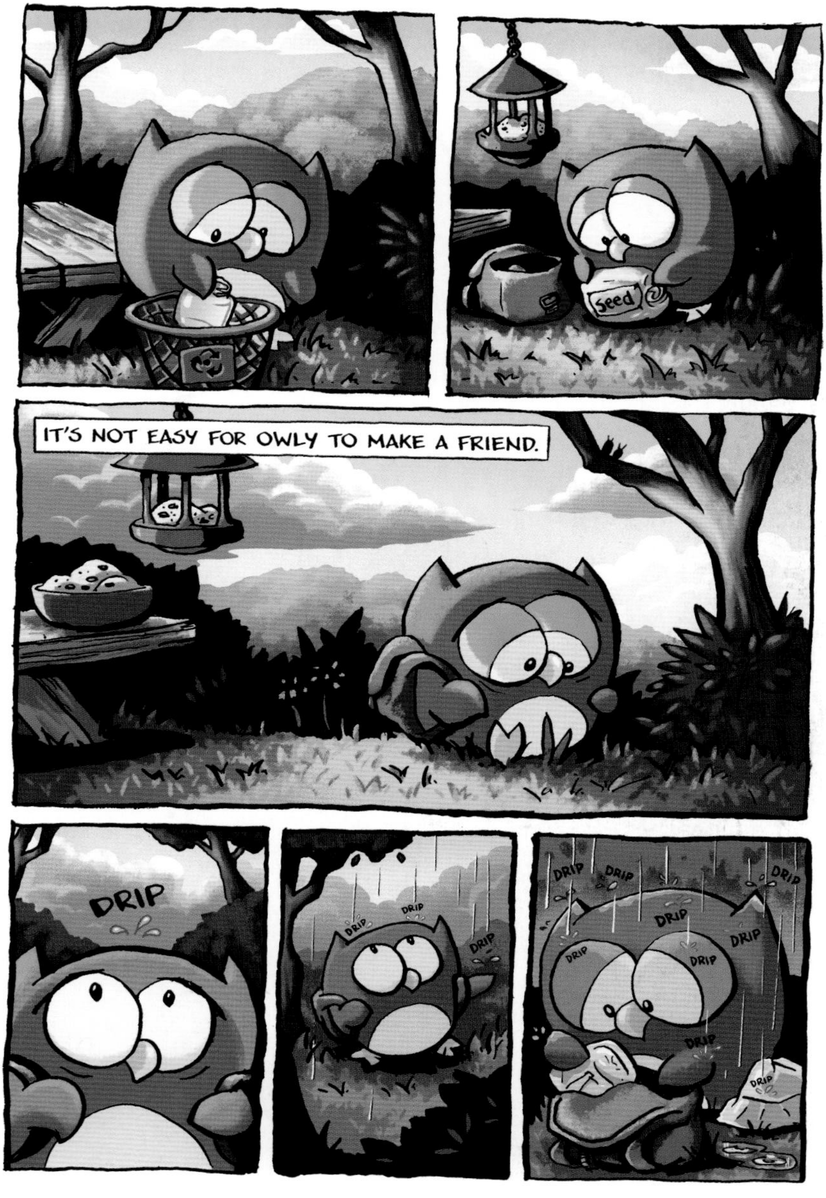
Seed
IT'S NOT EASY FOR OWLY TO MAKE A FRIEND.
DRIP
DRIP
DRIP
DRIP
DRIP
DRIP
DRIP
DRIP
DRIP
DRIP
DRIP
DRIP
DRIP
DRIP

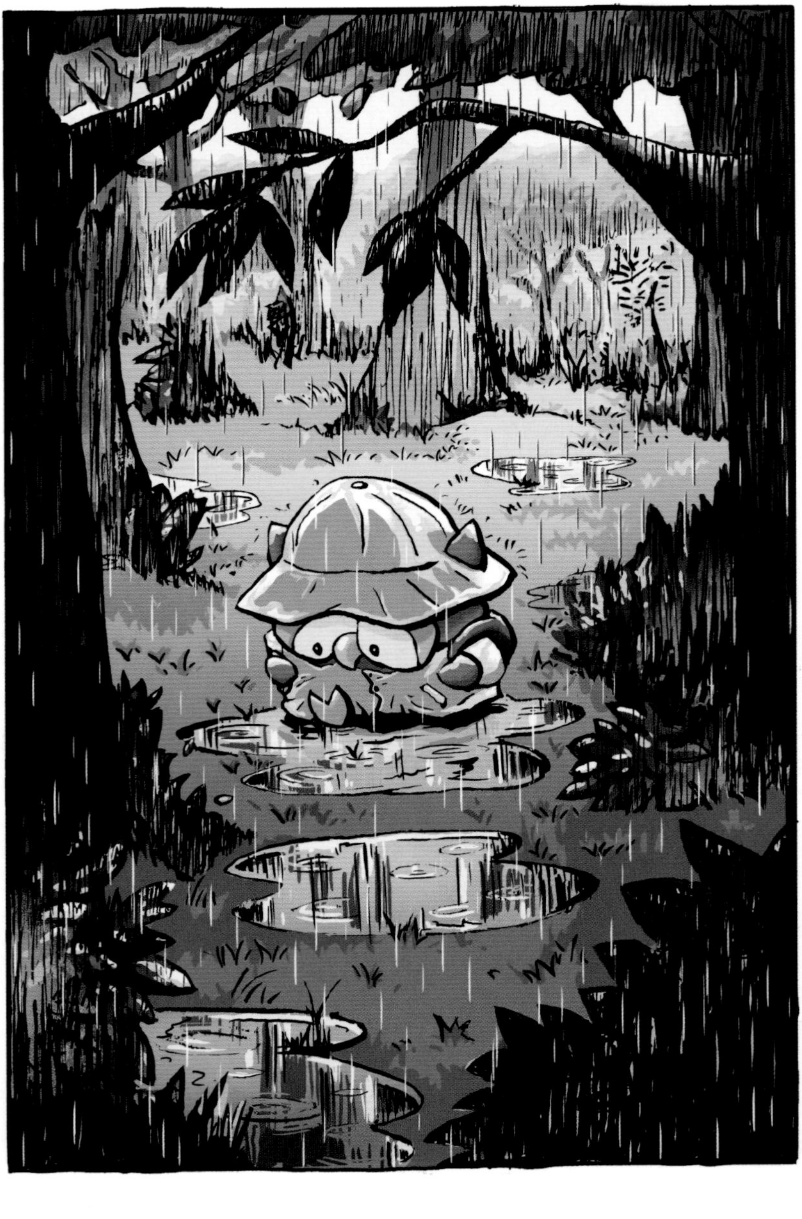

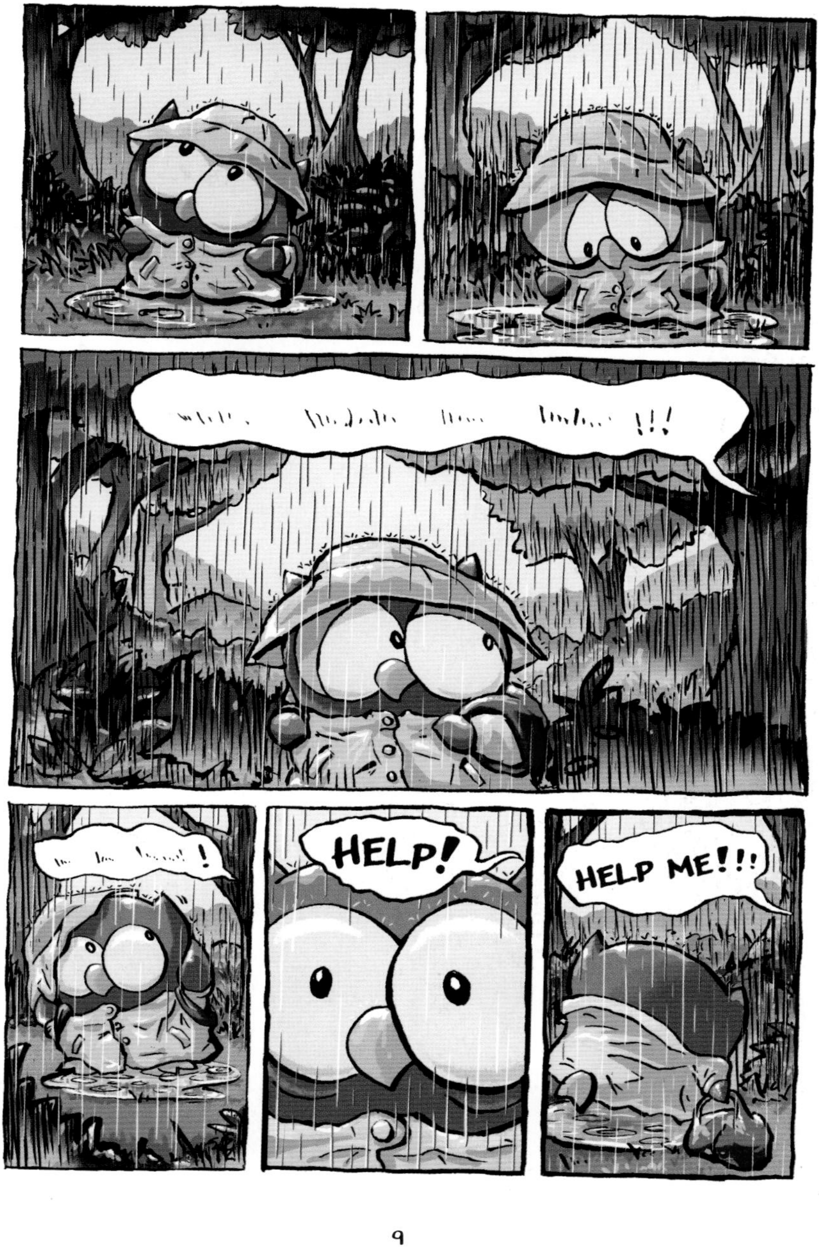
HELP!
HELP ME!!!

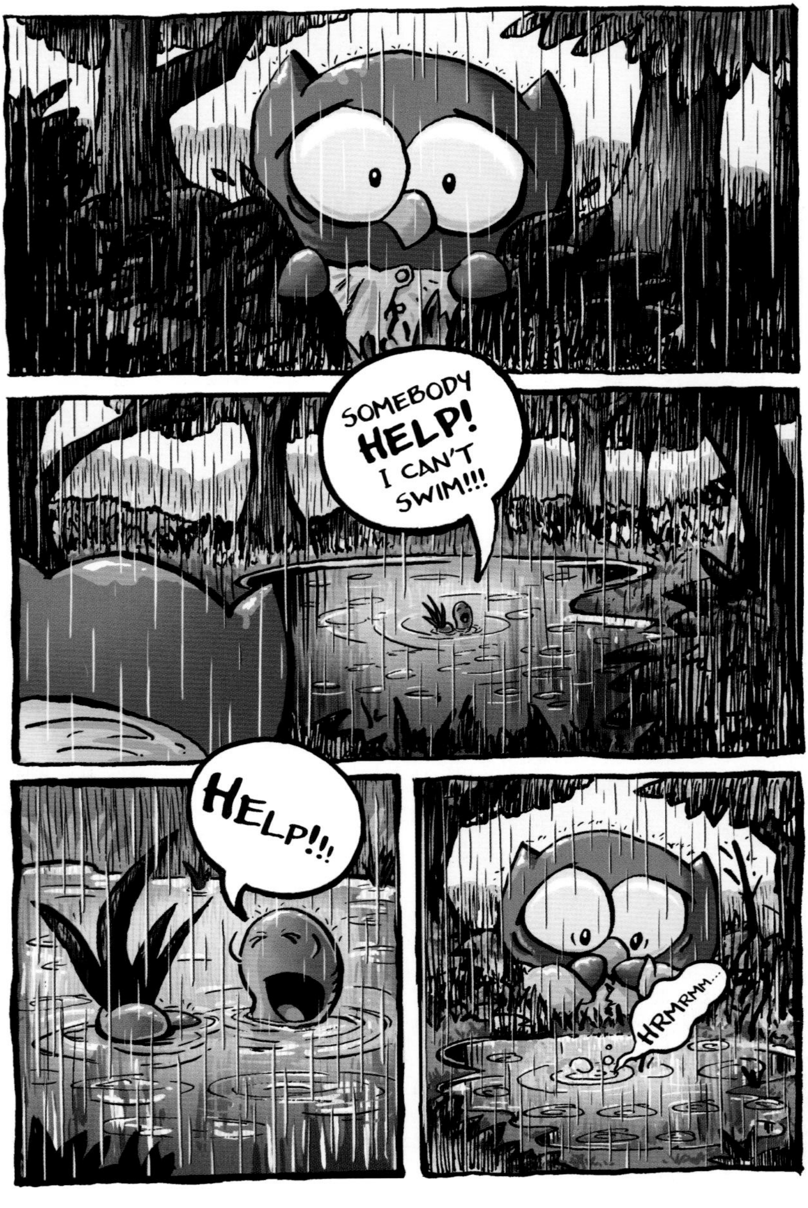
SOMEBODY HELP! I CAN'T SWIM!!!
HELP!!!
HRMRMM...

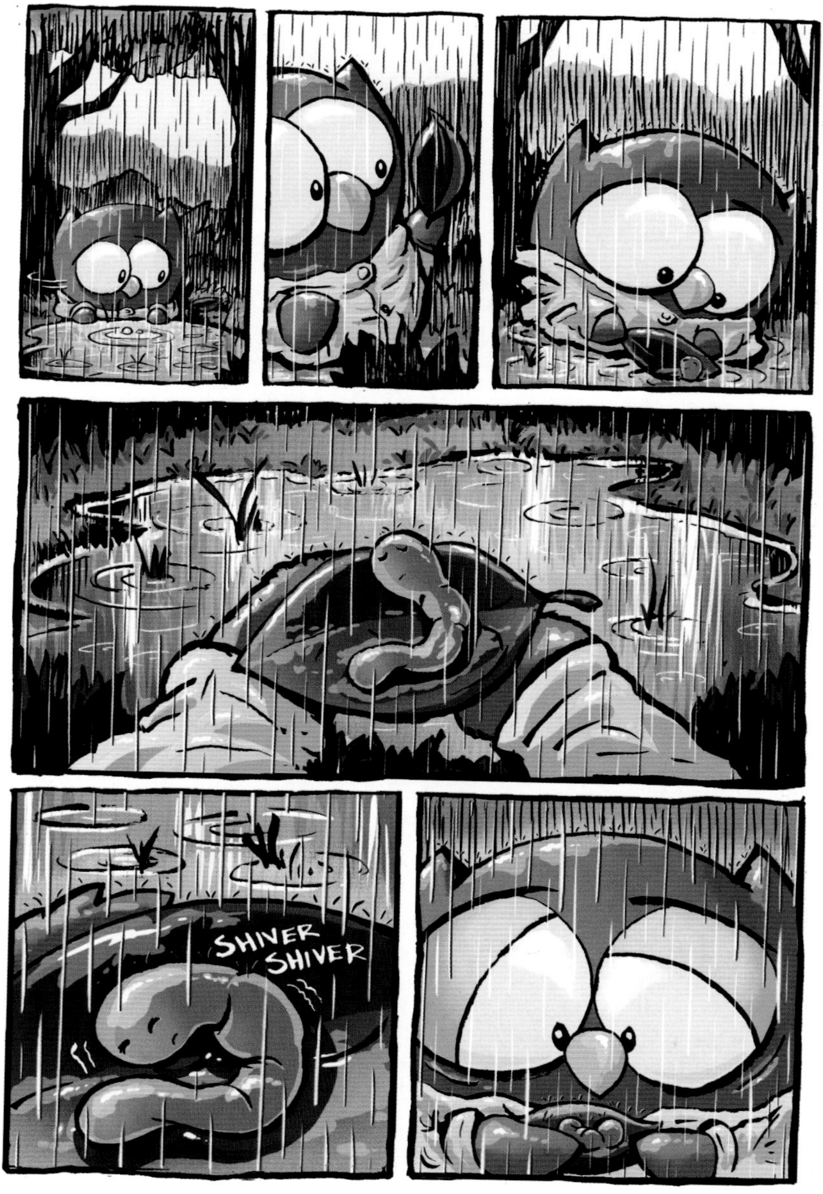
SHIVER
SHIVER

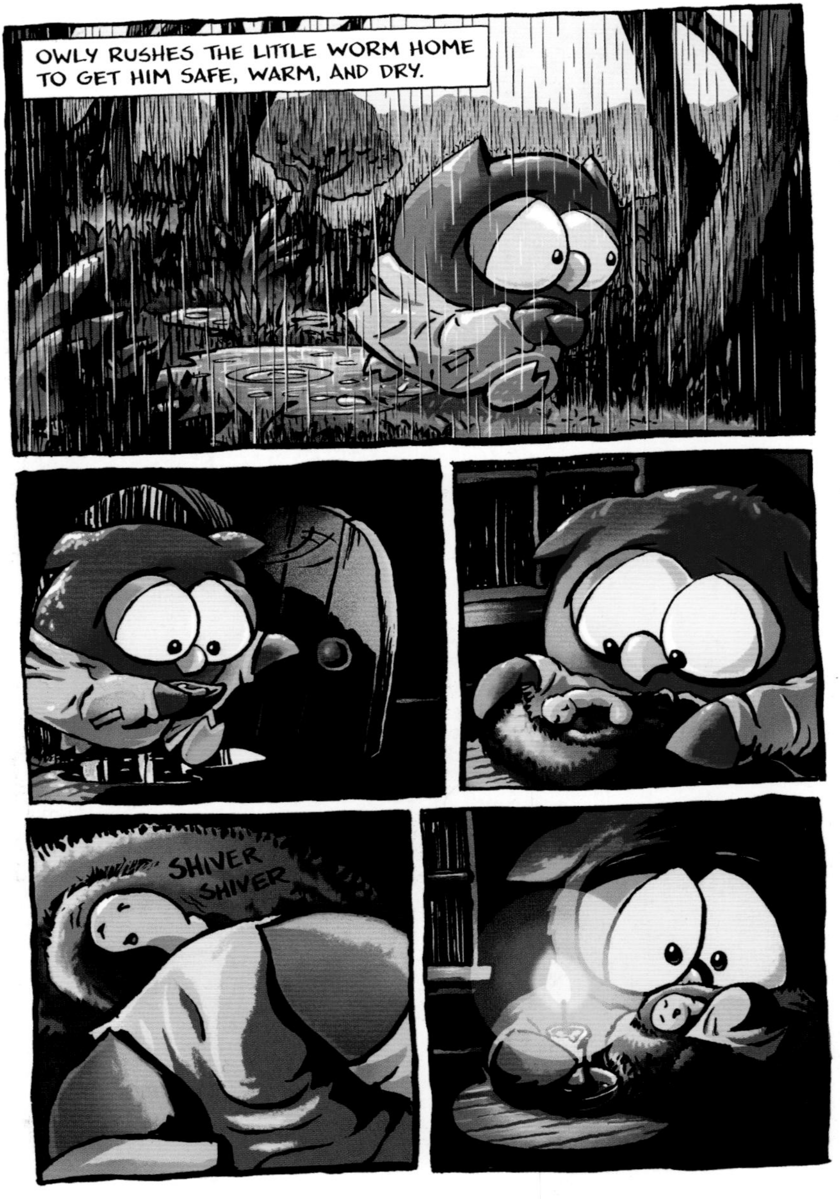
OWLY RUSHES THE LITTLE WORM HOME TO GET HIM SAFE, WARM, AND DRY.
SHIVER SHIVER

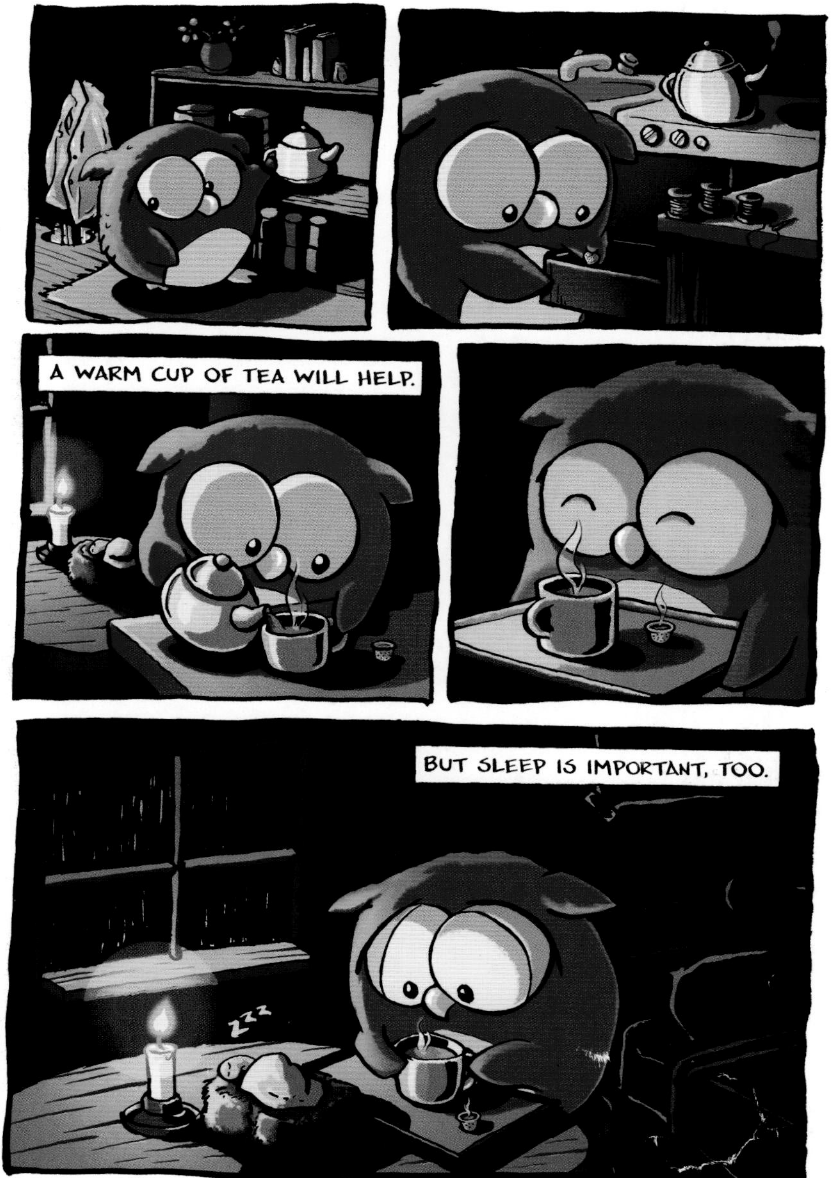
A WARM CUP OF TEA WILL HELP.
BUT SLEEP IS IMPORTANT, TOO.
zzz

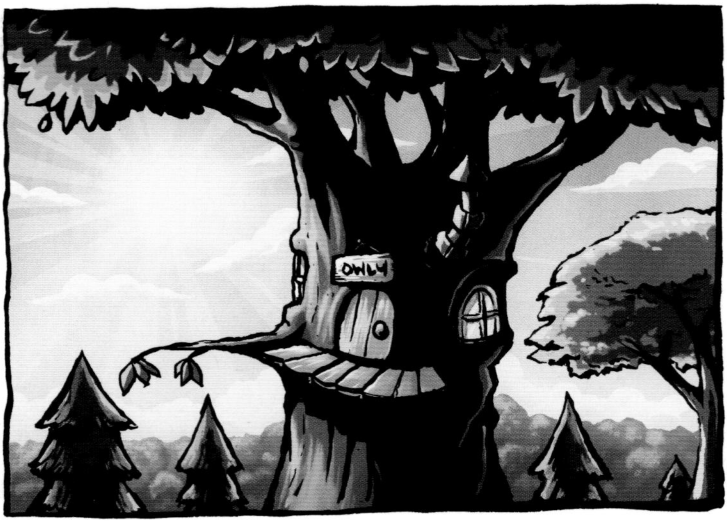
OWLY

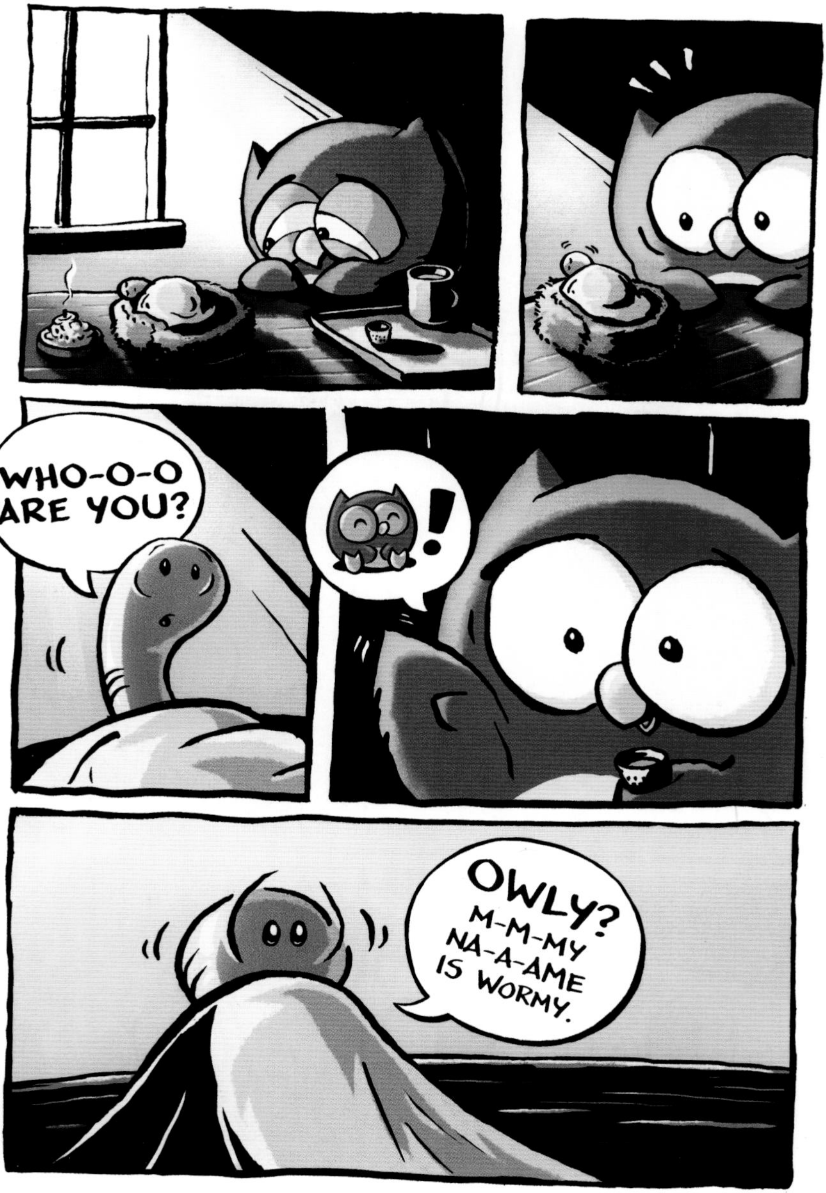
WHO-O-O ARE YOU?
!
OWLY? M-M-MY NA-A-AME IS WORMY.

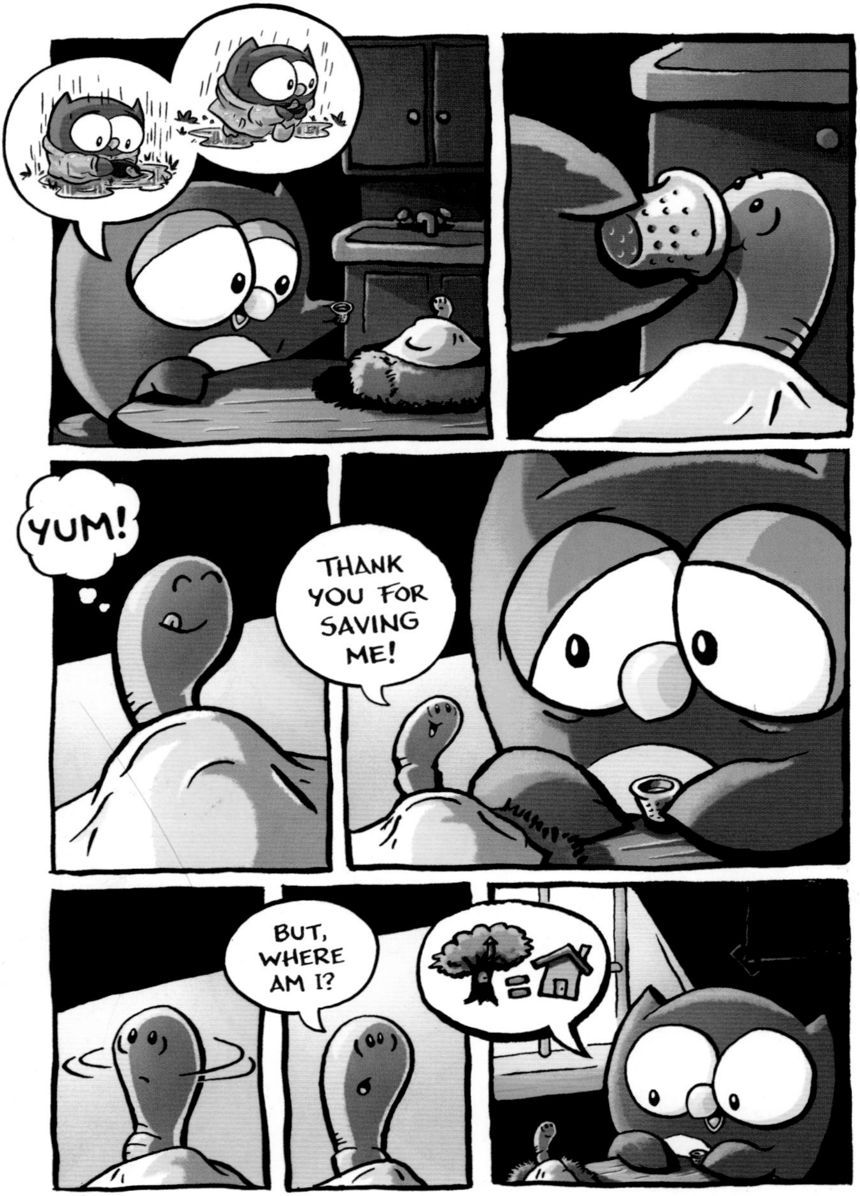
YUM!
THANK YOU FOR SAVING ME!
BUT, WHERE AM I?

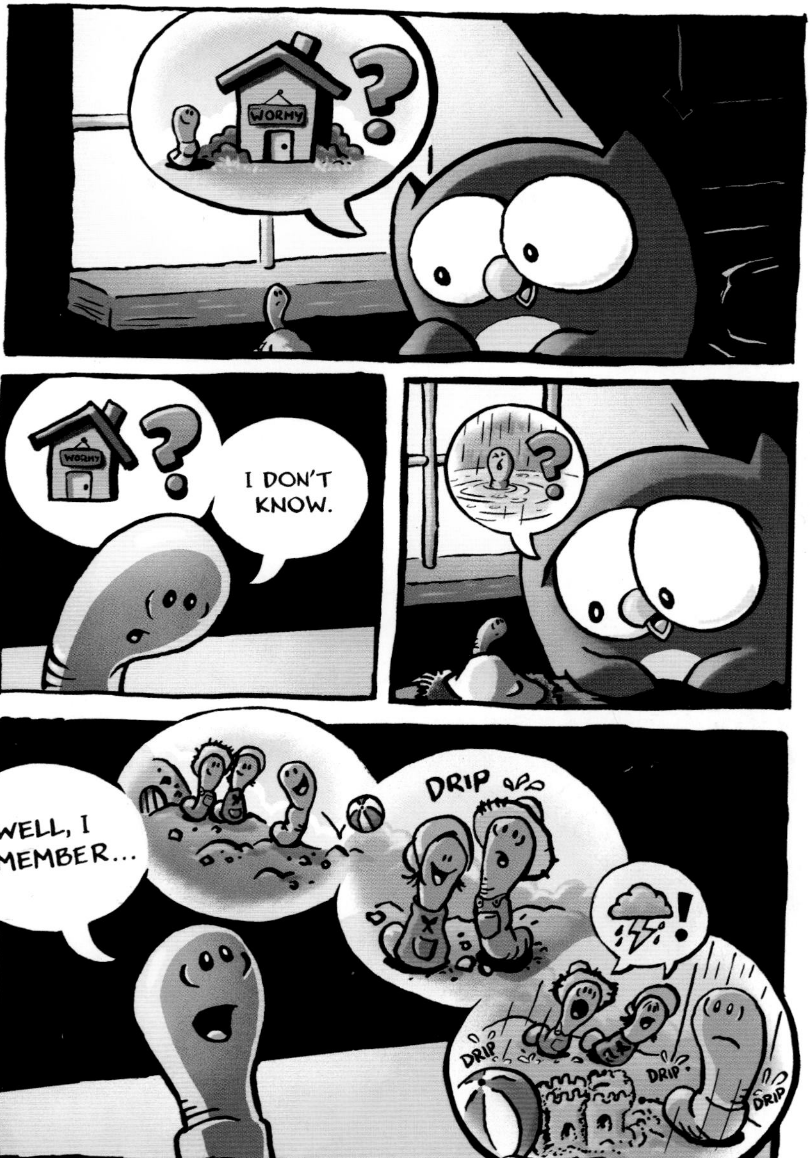
WORMY
WORMY
I DON'T KNOW.
WELL, I REMEMBER...
DRIP
DRIP
DRIP
DRIP

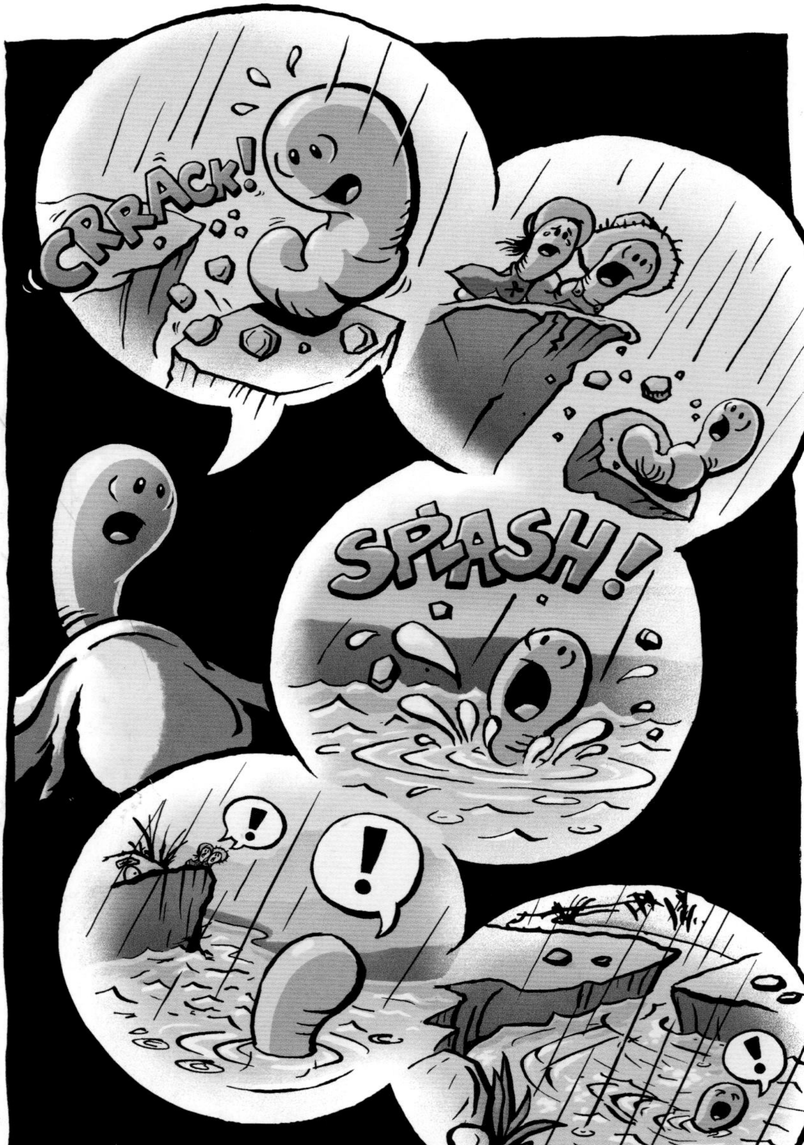
CRRACK!
SPLASH!
!
!
!

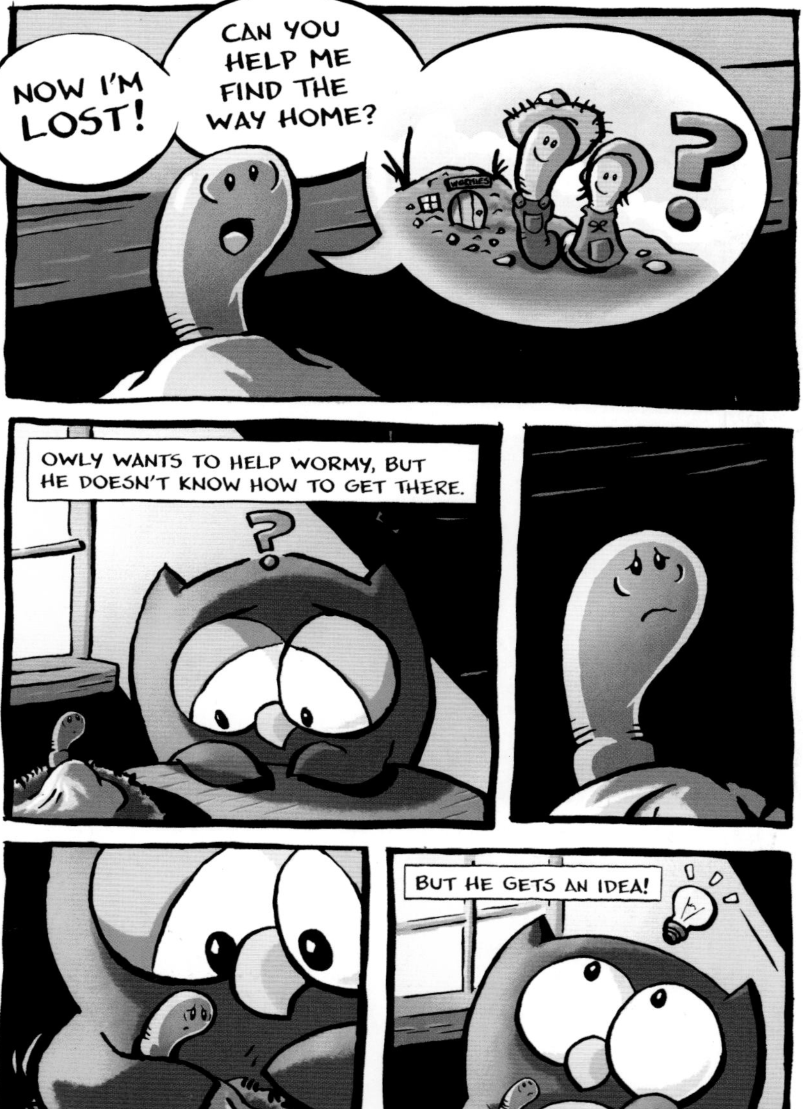
NOW I'M LOST!
CAN YOU HELP ME FIND THE WAY HOME?
OWLY WANTS TO HELP WORMY, BUT HE DOESN'T KNOW HOW TO GET THERE.
BUT HE GETS AN IDEA!

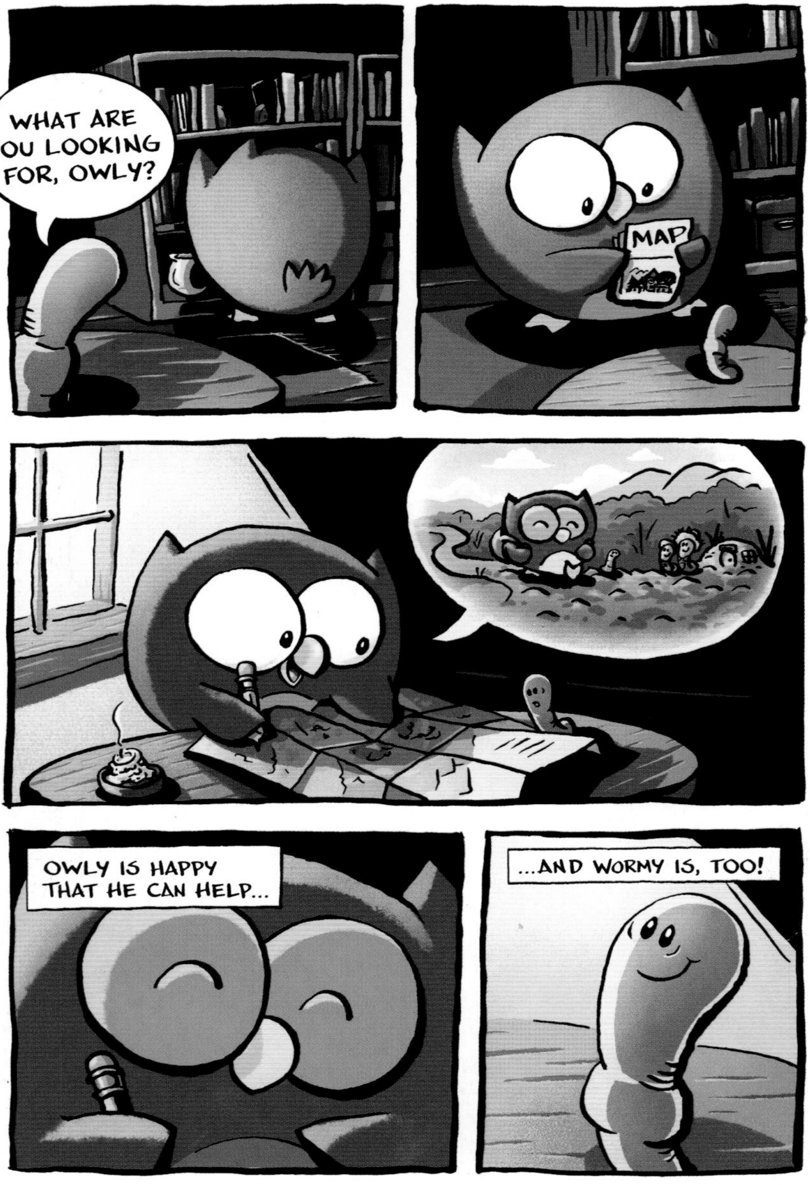
WHAT ARE YOU LOOKING FOR, OWLY?
MAP
OWLY IS HAPPY THAT HE CAN HELP...
...AND WORMY IS, TOO!

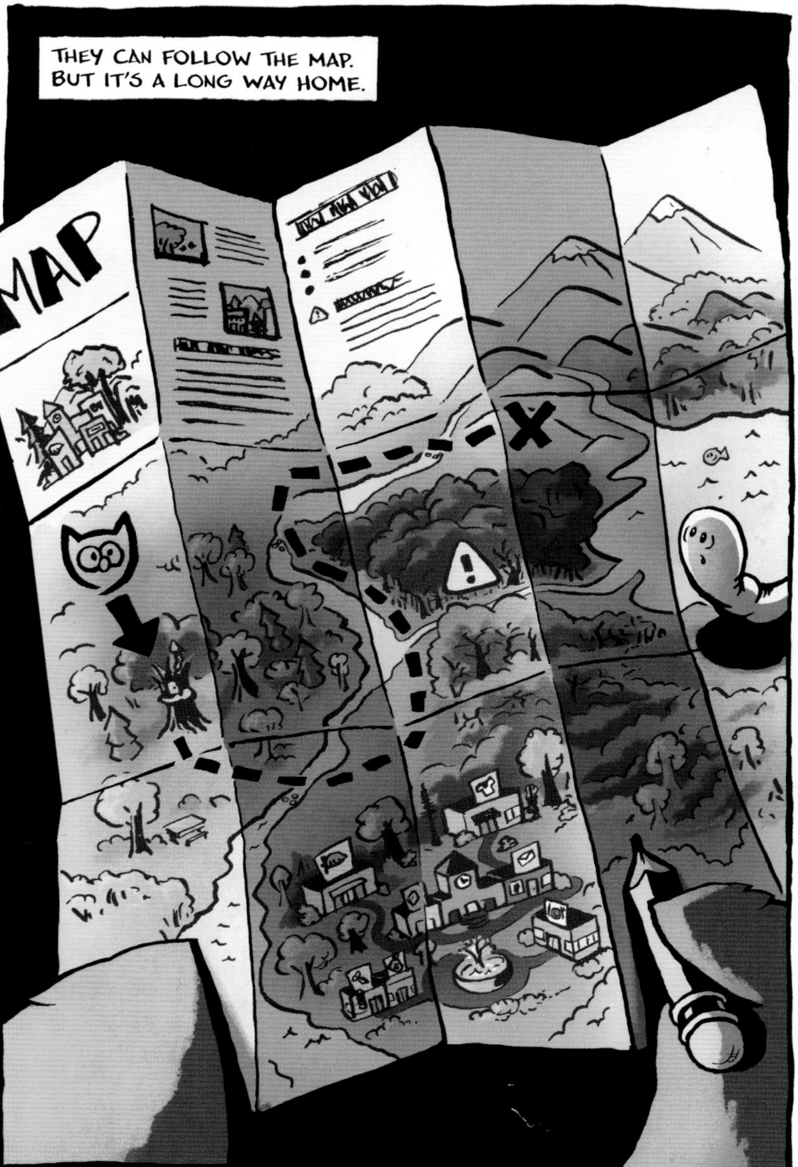
THEY CAN FOLLOW THE MAP. BUT IT'S A LONG WAY HOME.
MAP

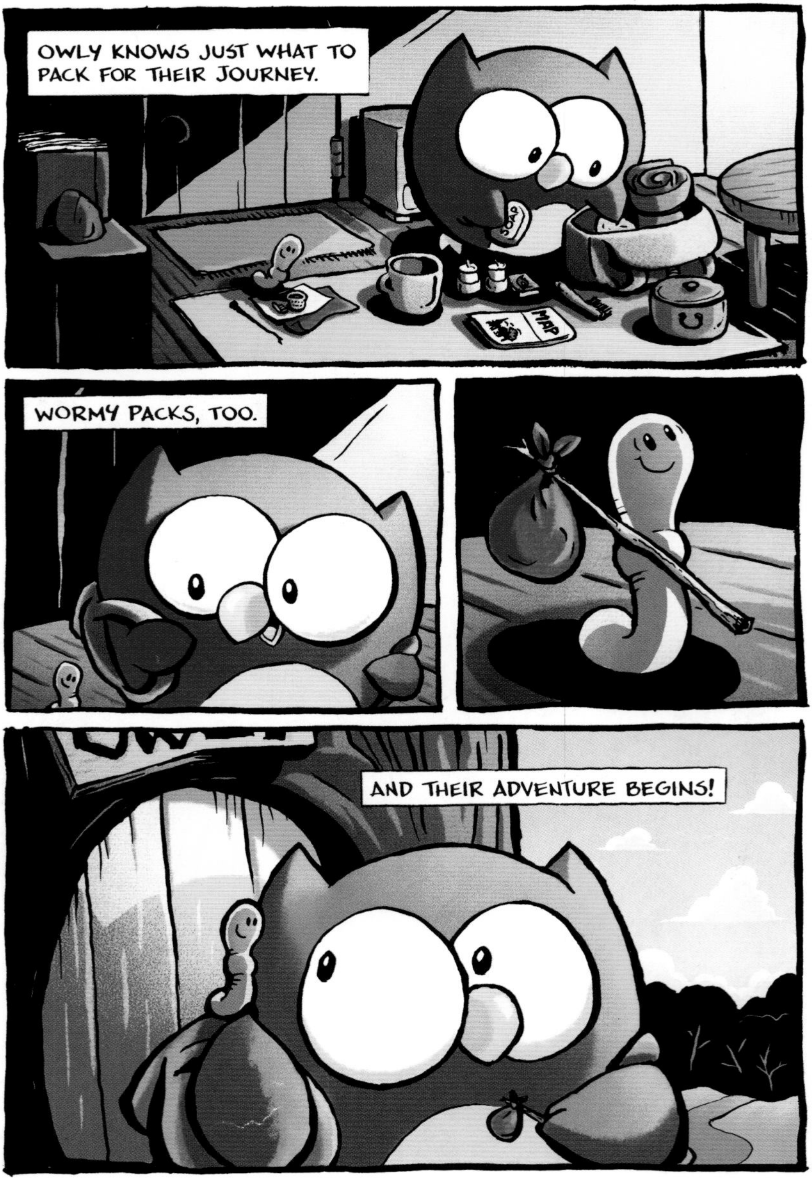
OWLY KNOWS JUST WHAT TO PACK FOR THEIR JOURNEY.
SOAP
MAP
WORMY PACKS, TOO.
AND THEIR ADVENTURE BEGINS!

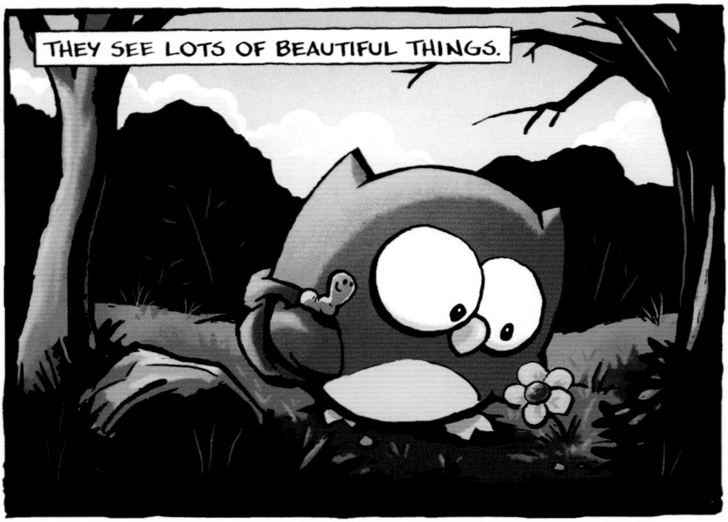
THEY SEE LOTS OF BEAUTIFUL THINGS.

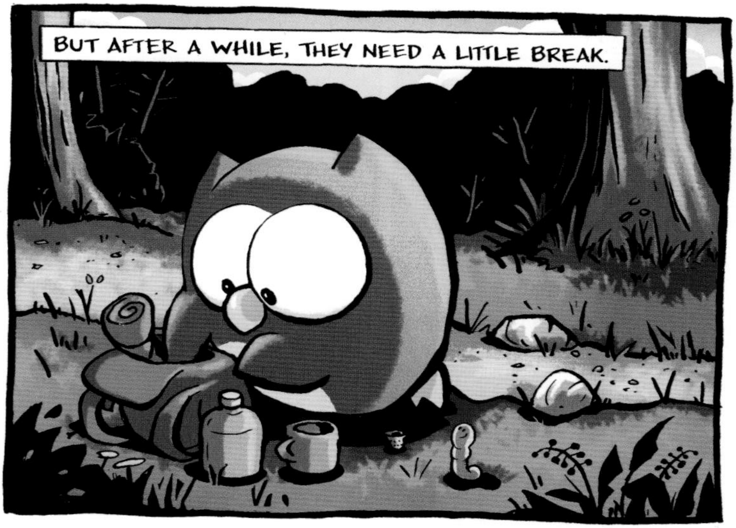
BUT AFTER A WHILE, THEY NEED A LITTLE BREAK.

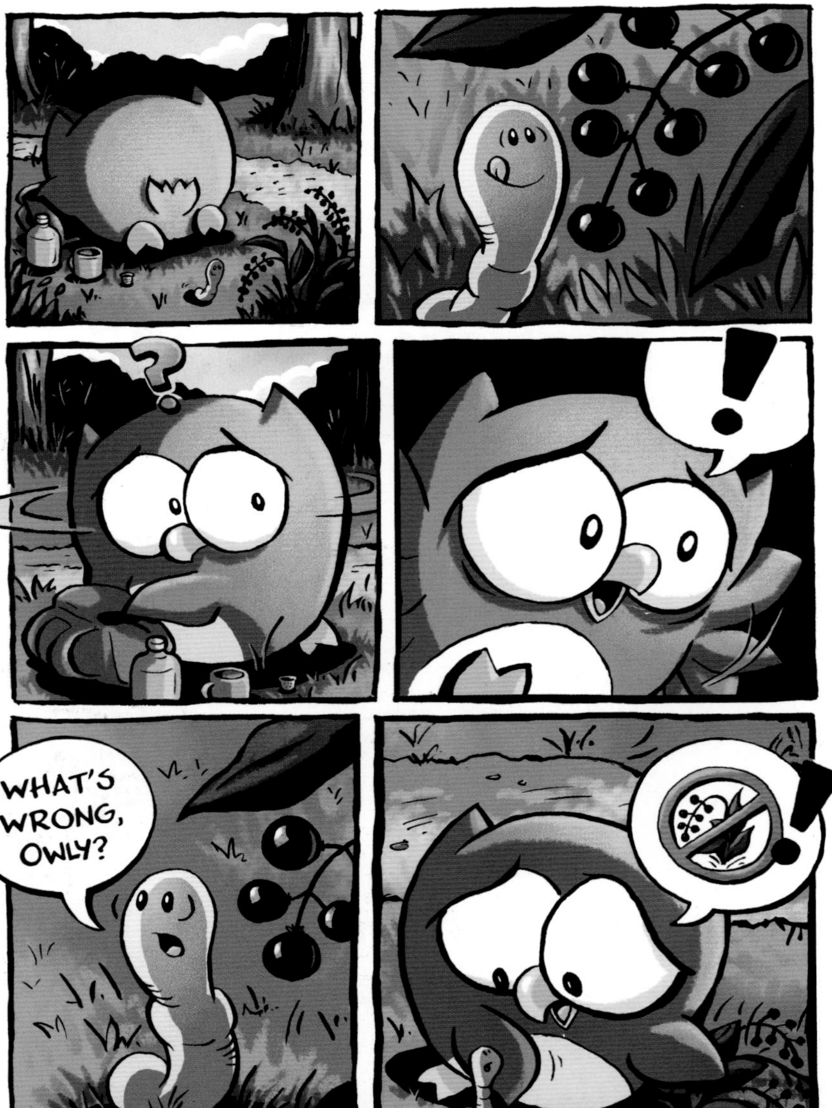
?
!
WHAT'S WRONG, OWLY?
!

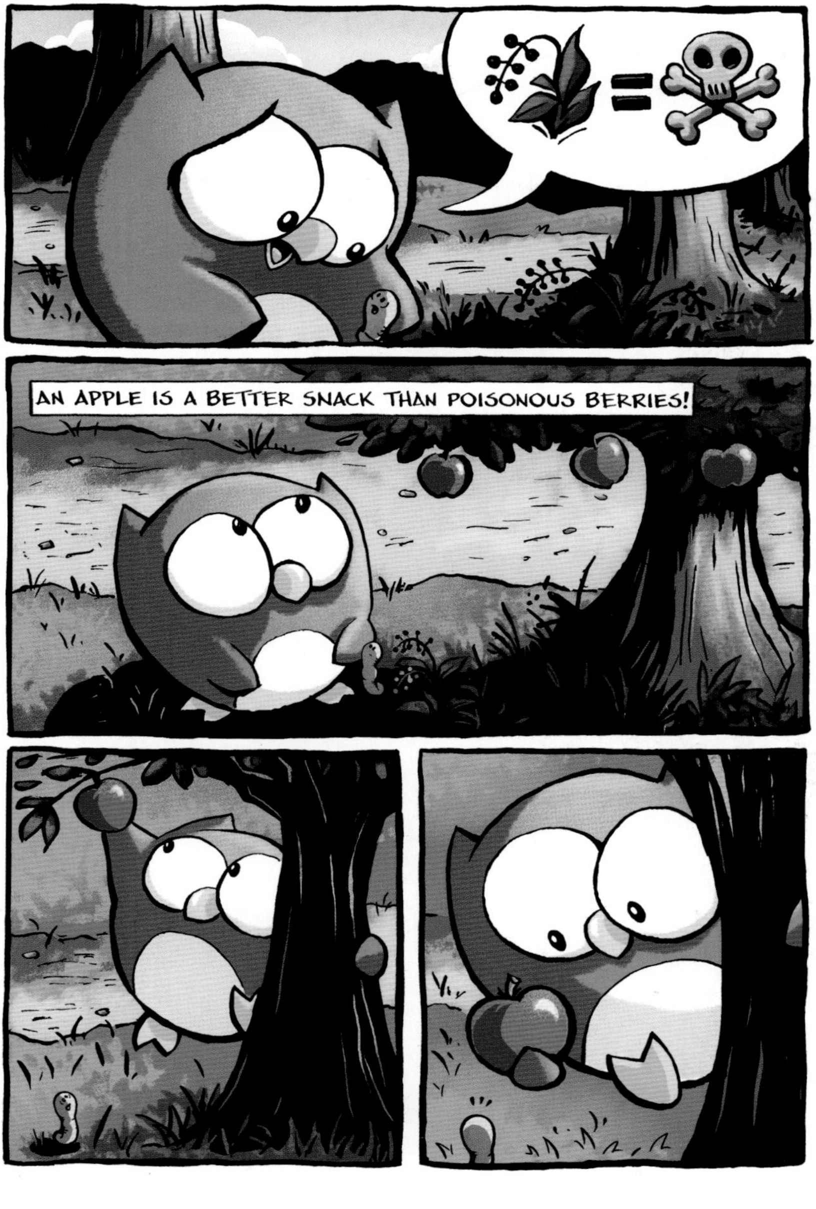
AN APPLE IS A BETTER SNACK THAN POISONOUS BERRIES!

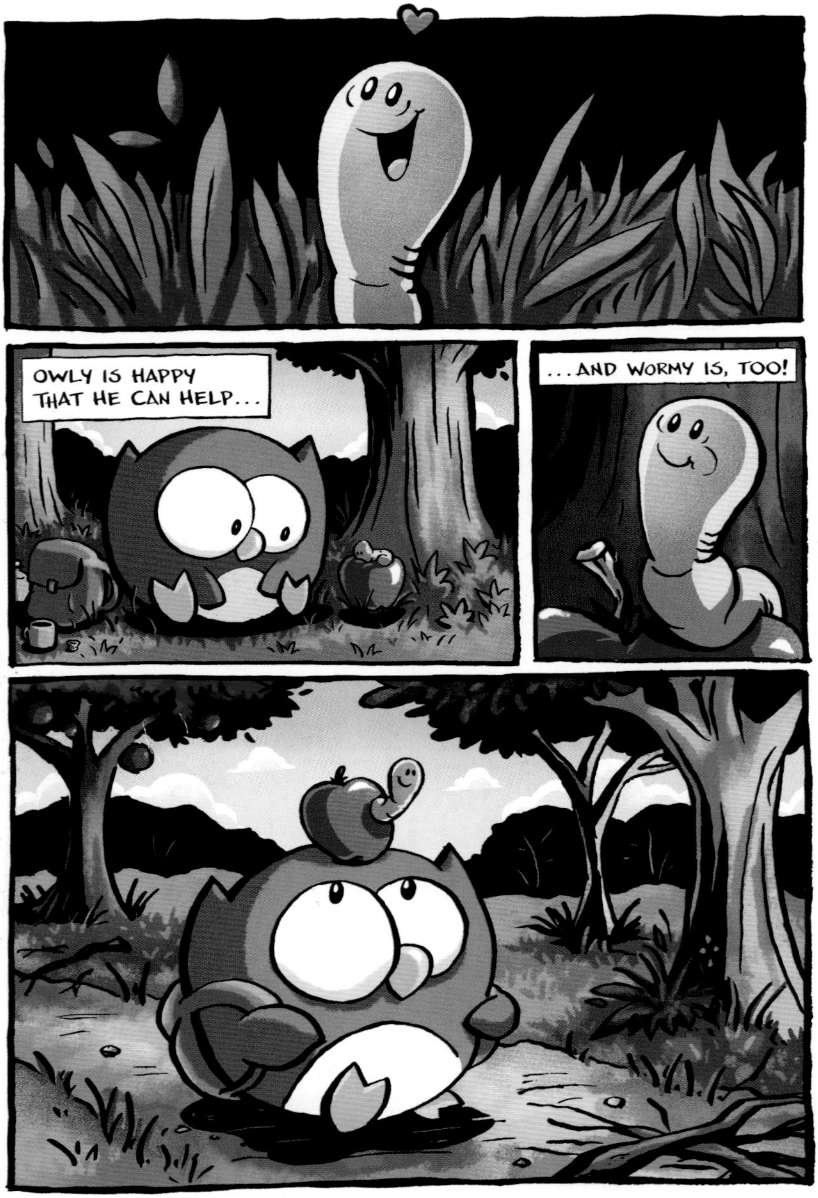
OWLY IS HAPPY THAT HE CAN HELP...
...AND WORMY IS, TOO!

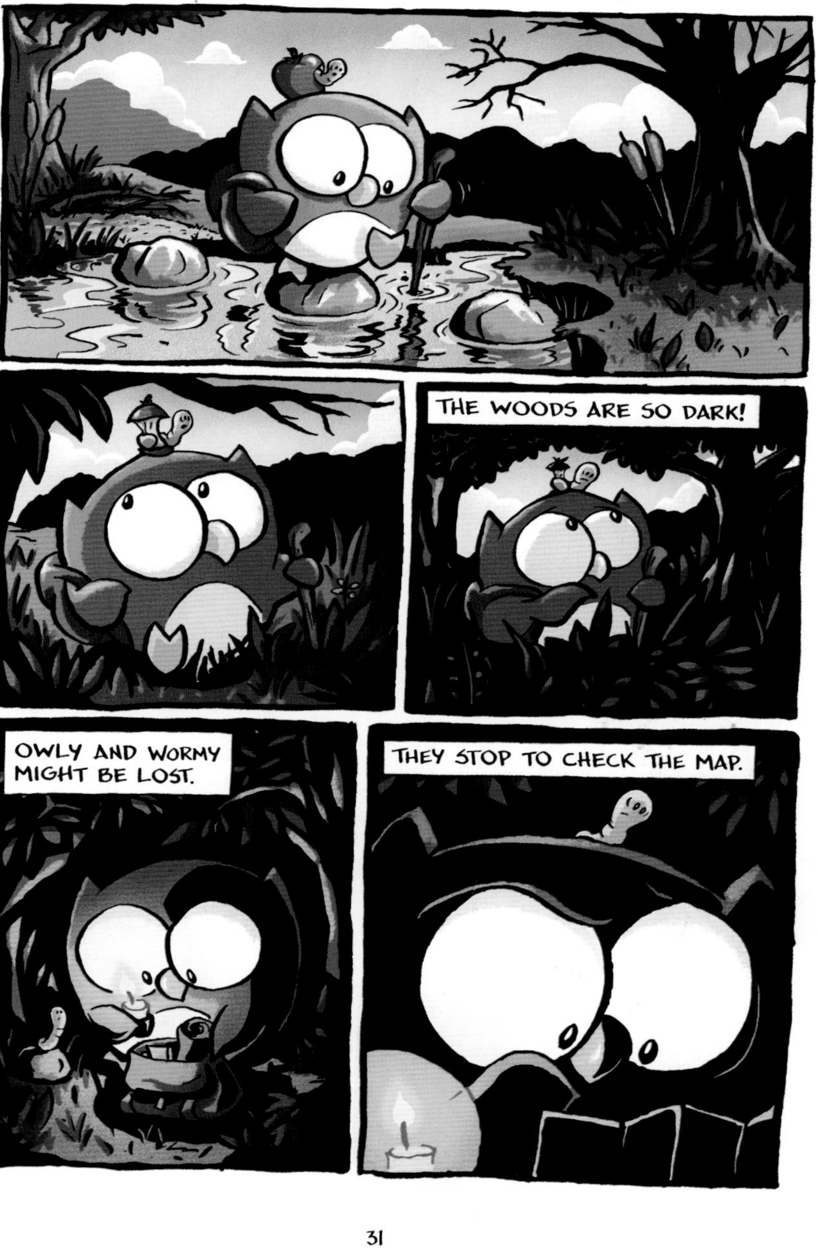
THE WOODS ARE SO DARK!
OWLY AND WORMY MIGHT BE LOST.
THEY STOP TO CHECK THE MAP.

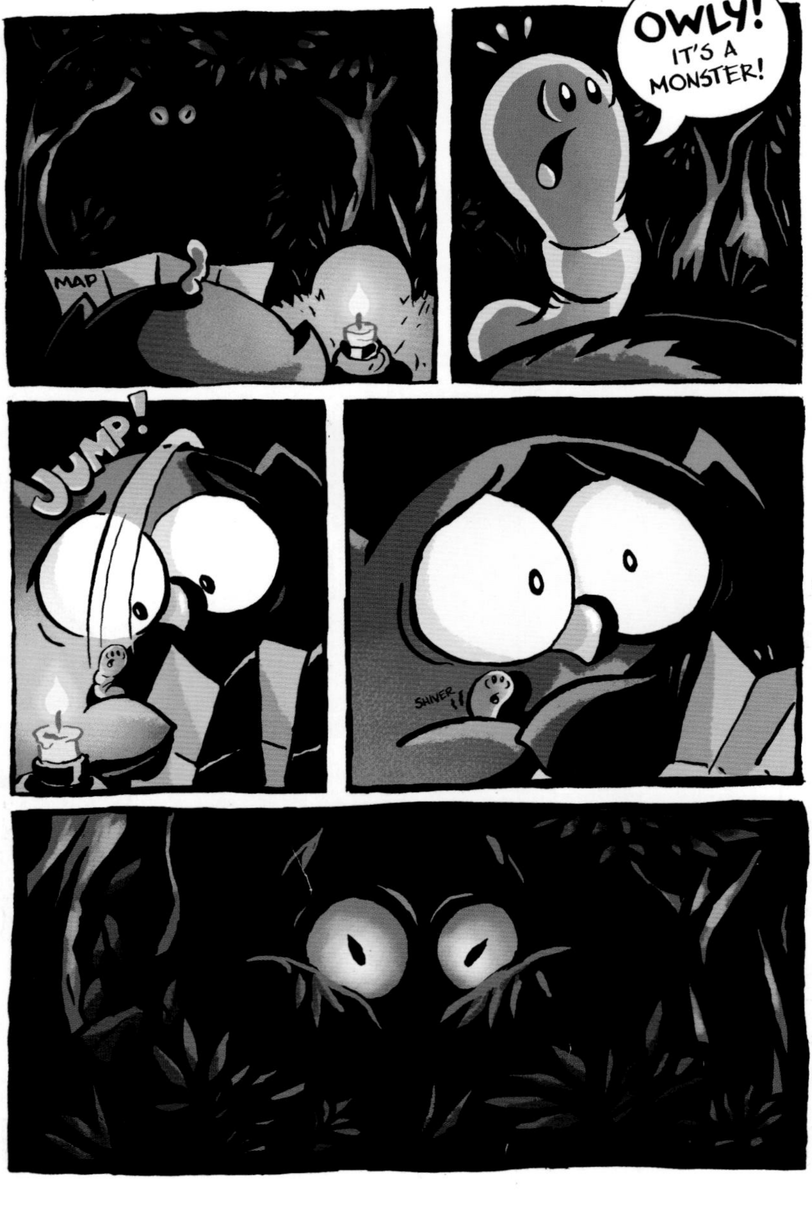
MAP
OWLY! IT'S A MONSTER!
JUMP!
SHIVER

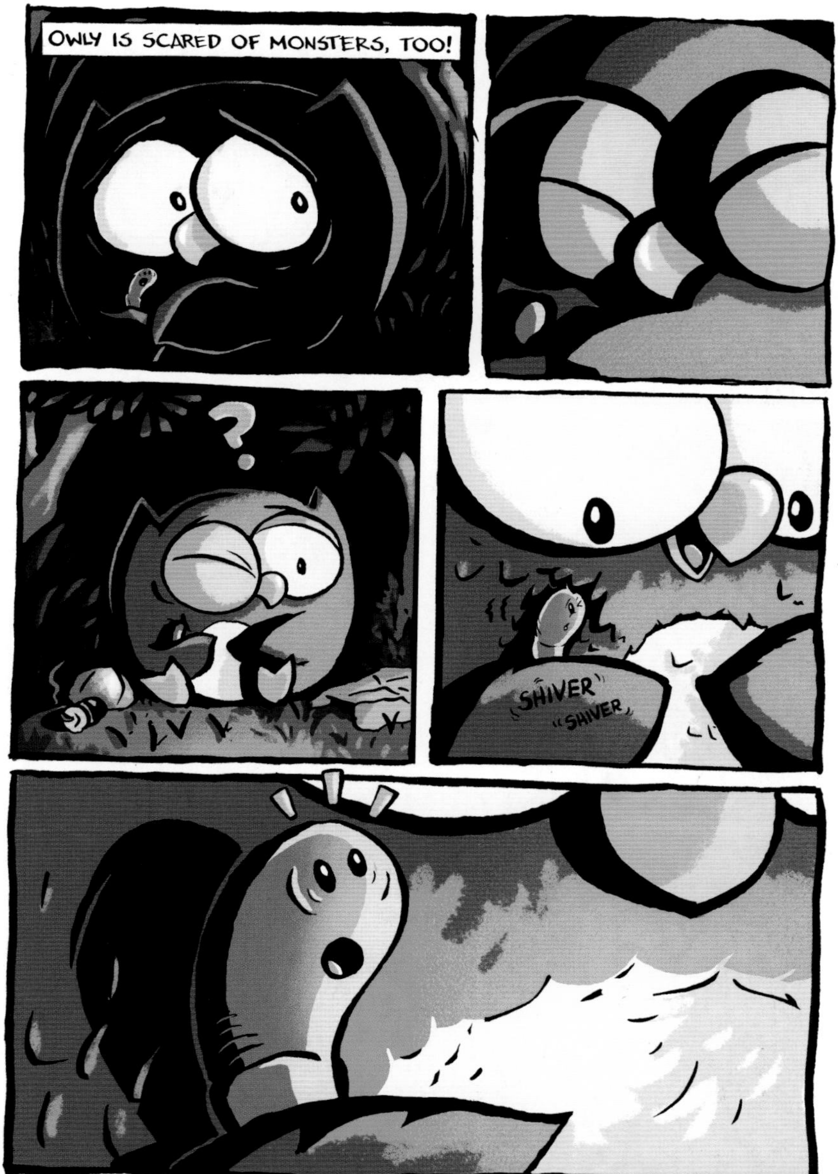
OWLY IS SCARED OF MONSTERS, TOO!
?
SHIVER
SHIVER

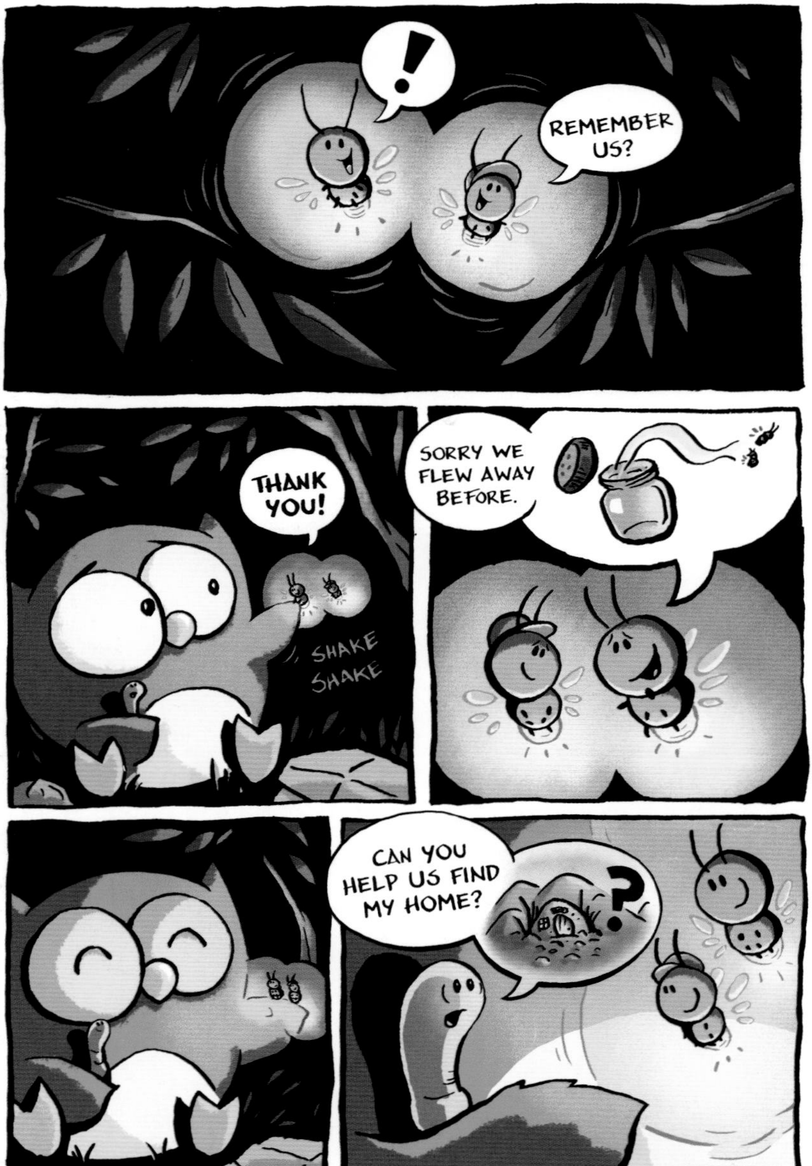
!
REMEMBER US?
THANK YOU!
SHAKE SHAKE
SORRY WE FLEW AWAY BEFORE.
CAN YOU HELP US FIND MY HOME?
?

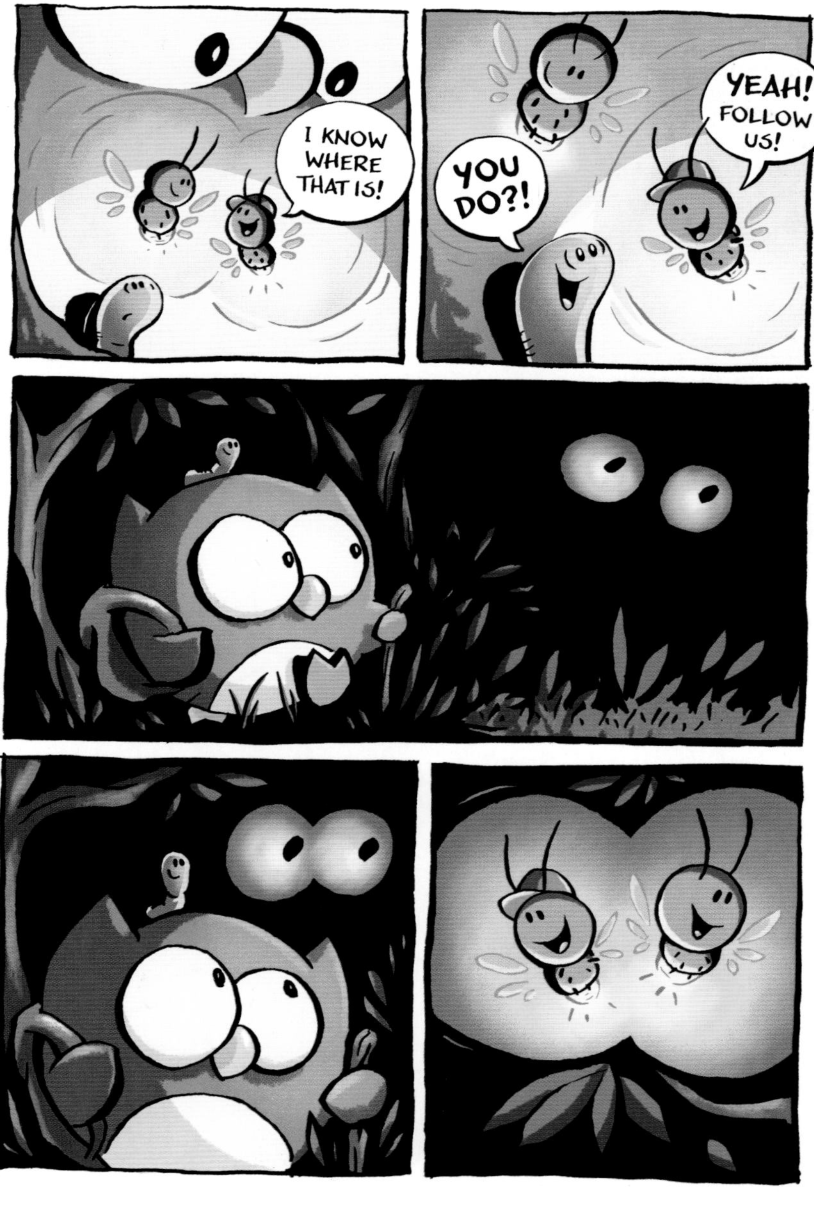
I KNOW WHERE THAT IS!
YOU DO?!
YEAH! FOLLOW US!

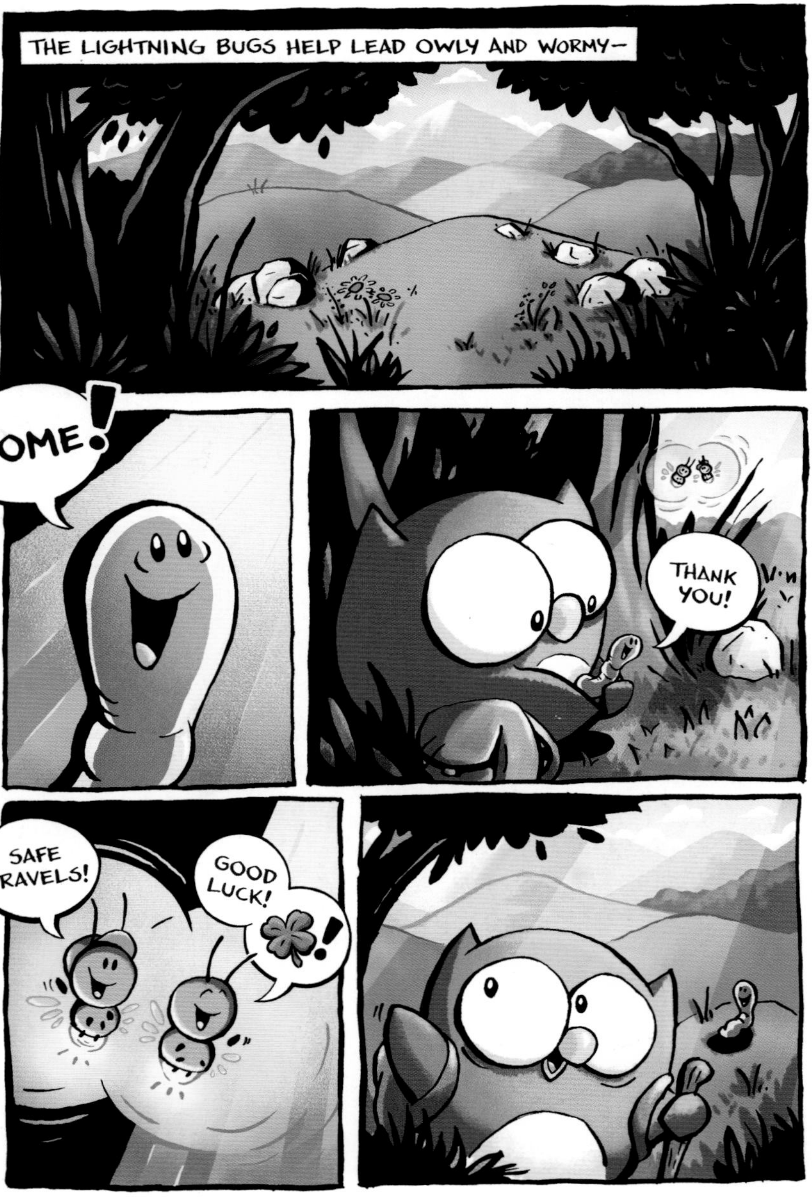
THE LIGHTNING BUGS HELP LEAD OWLY AND WORMY—
HOME!
THANK YOU!
SAFE TRAVELS!
GOOD LUCK!

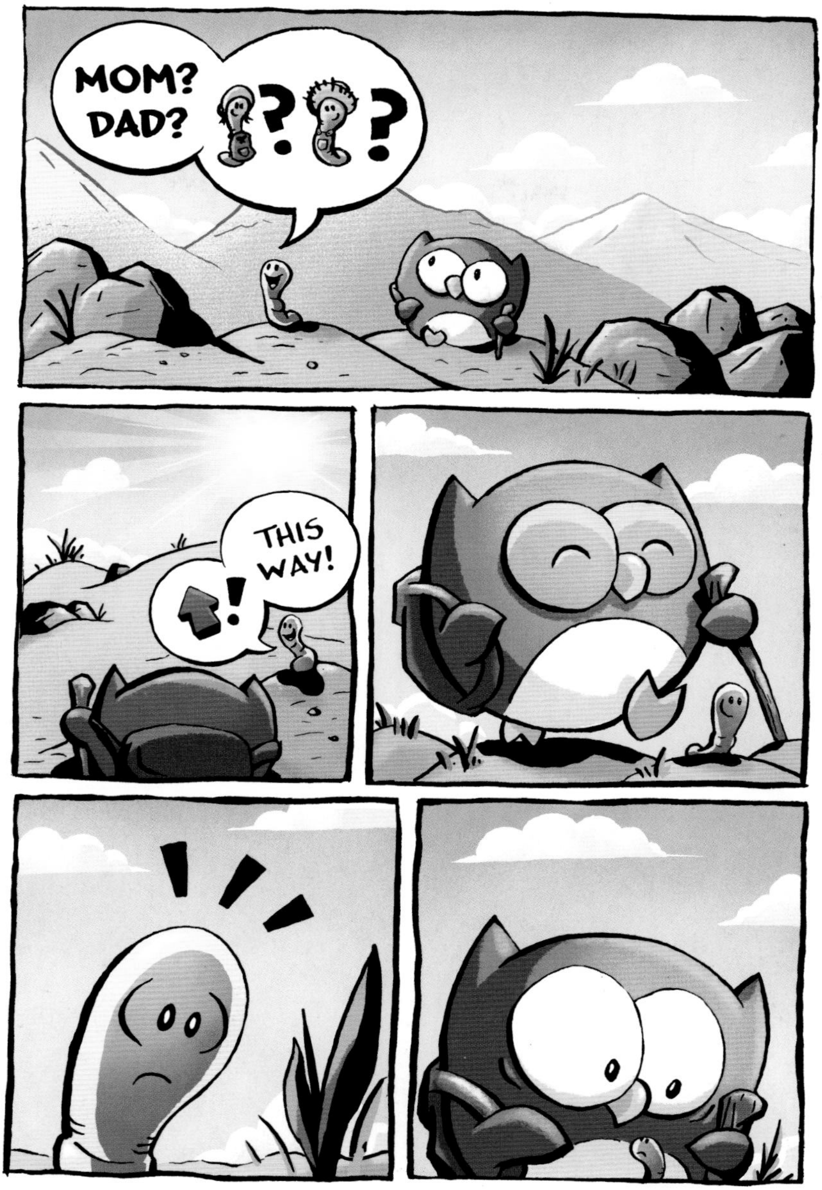
MOM? DAD?
THIS WAY!

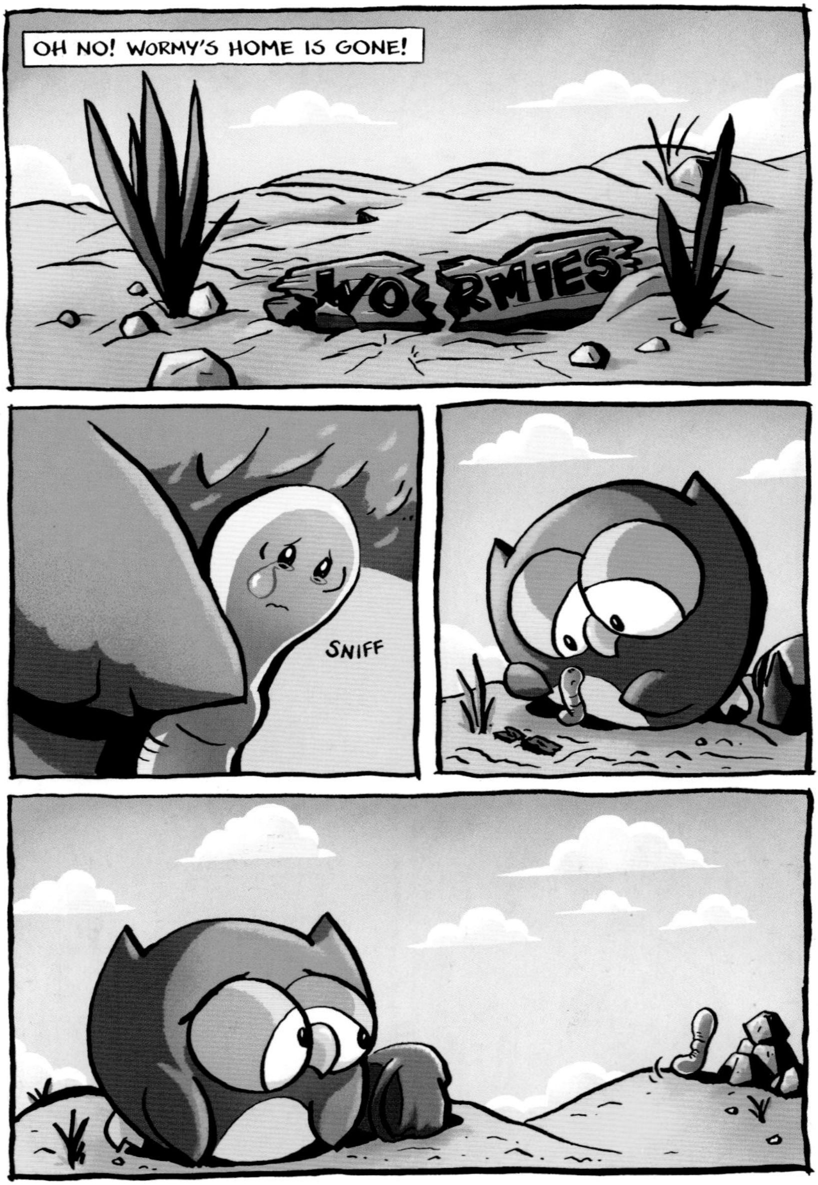
OH NO! WORMY'S HOME IS GONE!
WORMIES
SNIFF

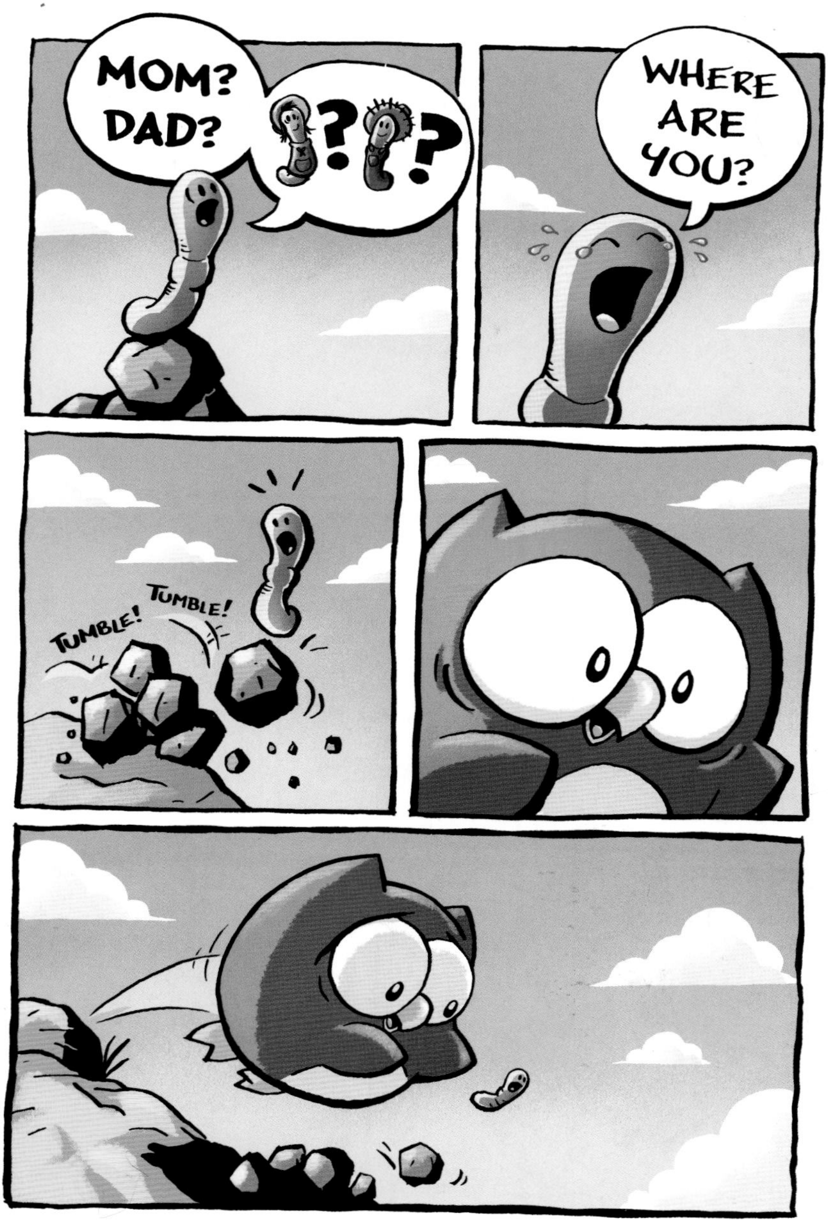
MOM?
DAD?
??
WHERE ARE YOU?
TUMBLE!
TUMBLE!

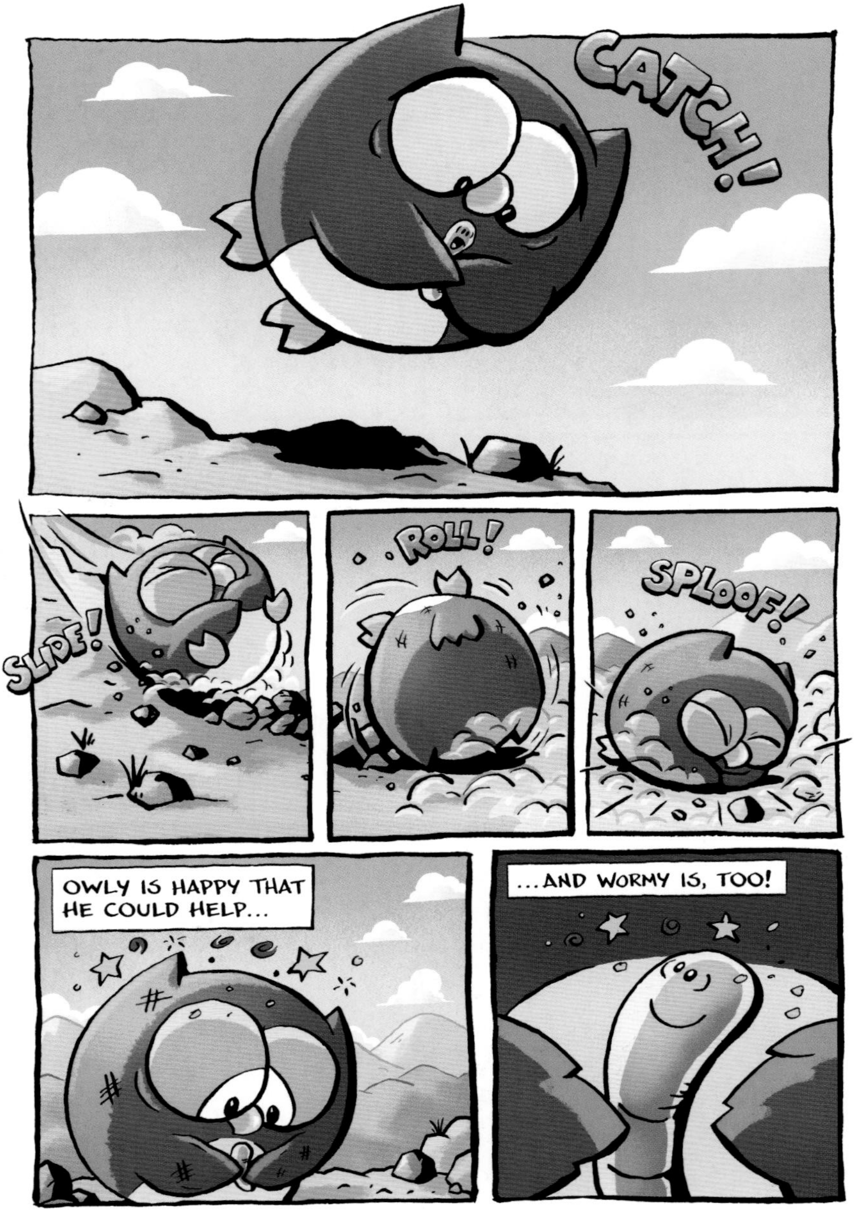
CATCH!
SLIDE!
ROLL!
SPLOOF!
OWLY IS HAPPY THAT HE COULD HELP...
...AND WORMY IS, TOO!

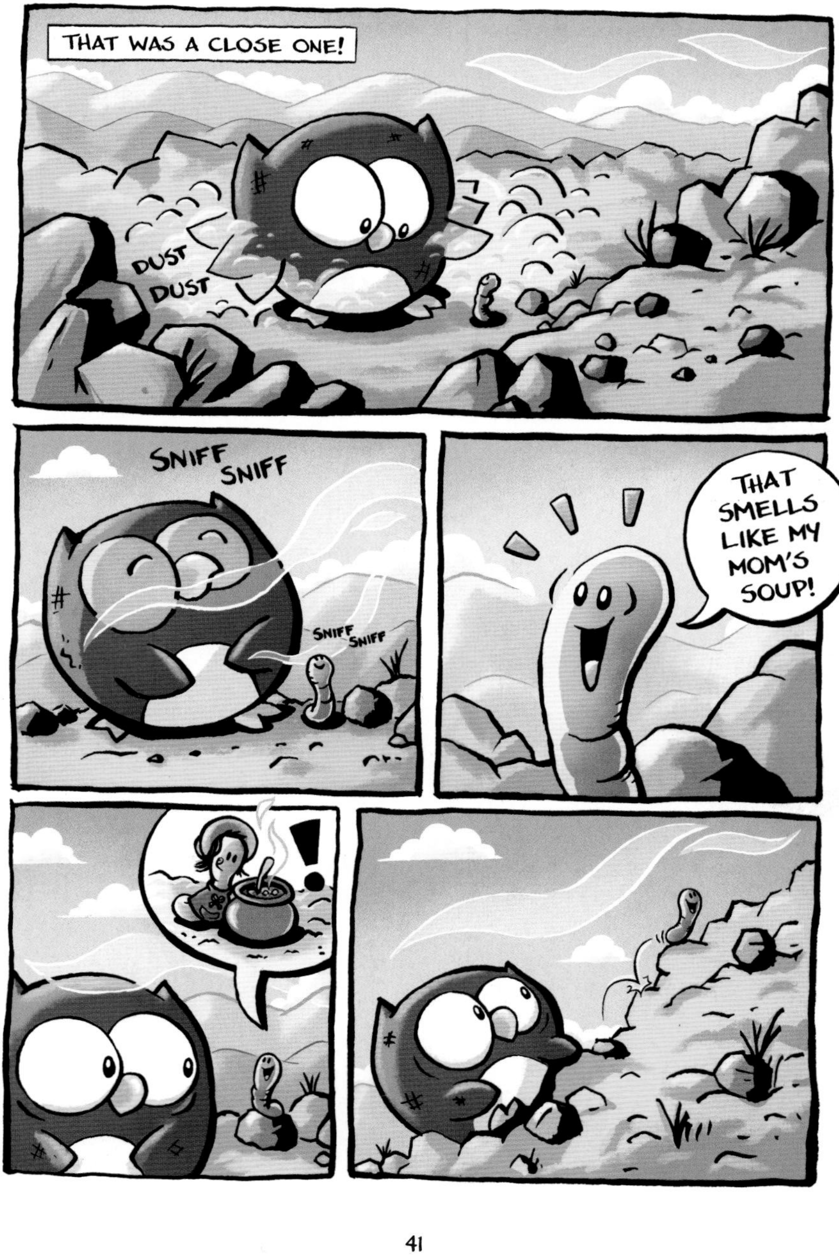
THAT WAS A CLOSE ONE!
DUST
DUST
SNIFF
SNIFF
SNIFF
SNIFF
THAT SMELLS LIKE MY MOM'S SOUP!
!

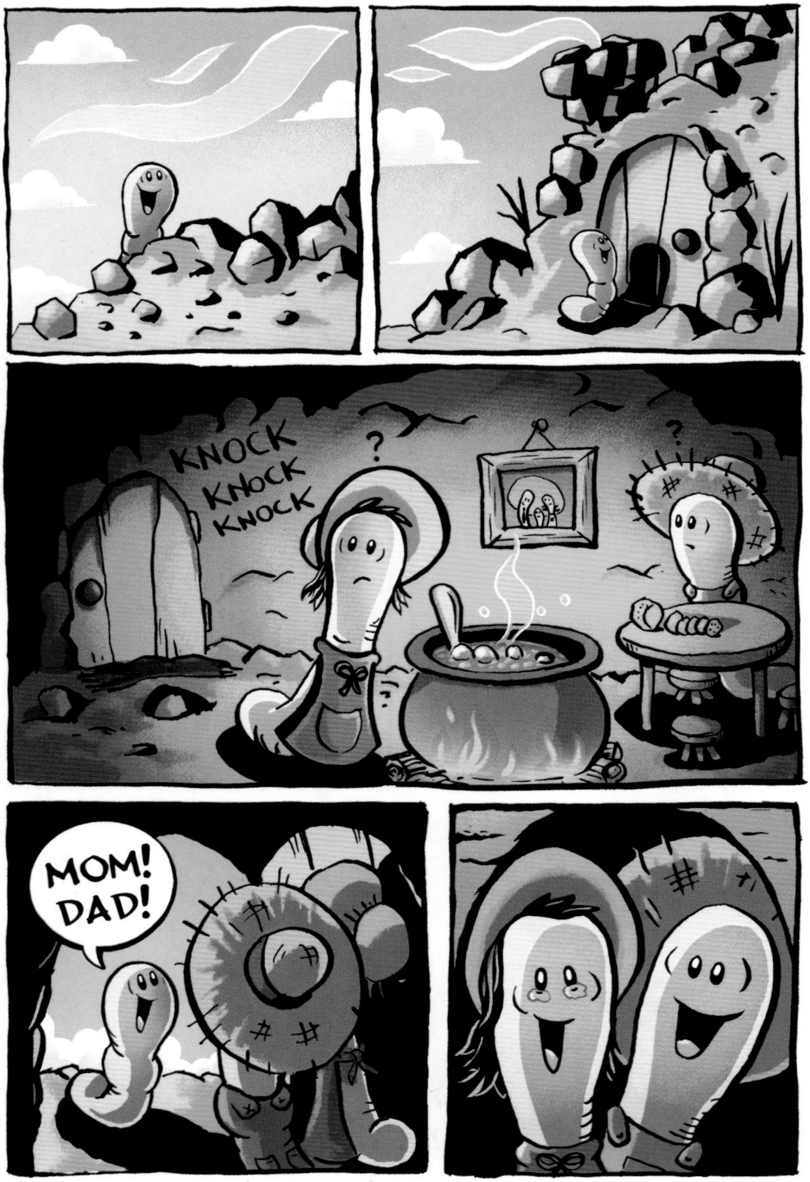
KNOCK
KNOCK
KNOCK
?
?
MOM! DAD!

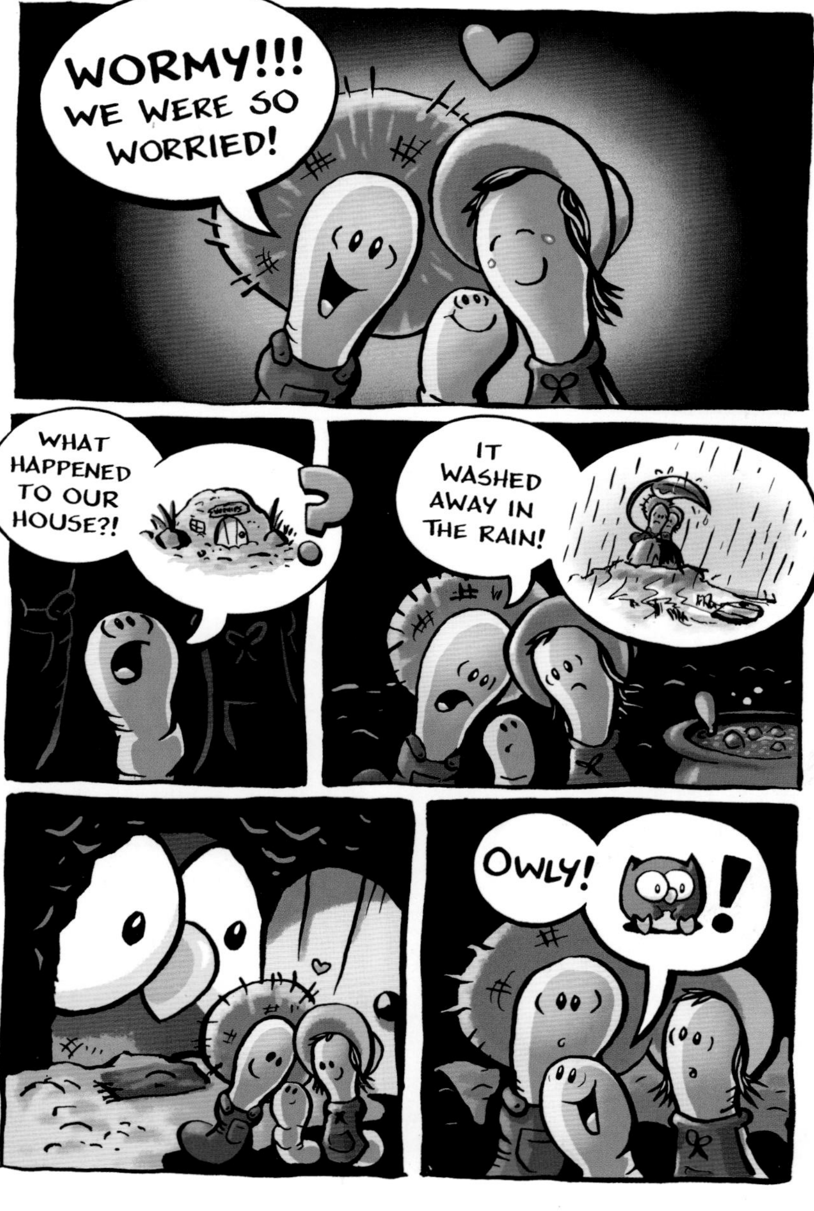
WORMY!!! WE WERE SO WORRIED!
WHAT HAPPENED TO OUR HOUSE?!
?
IT WASHED AWAY IN THE RAIN!
OWLY!
!

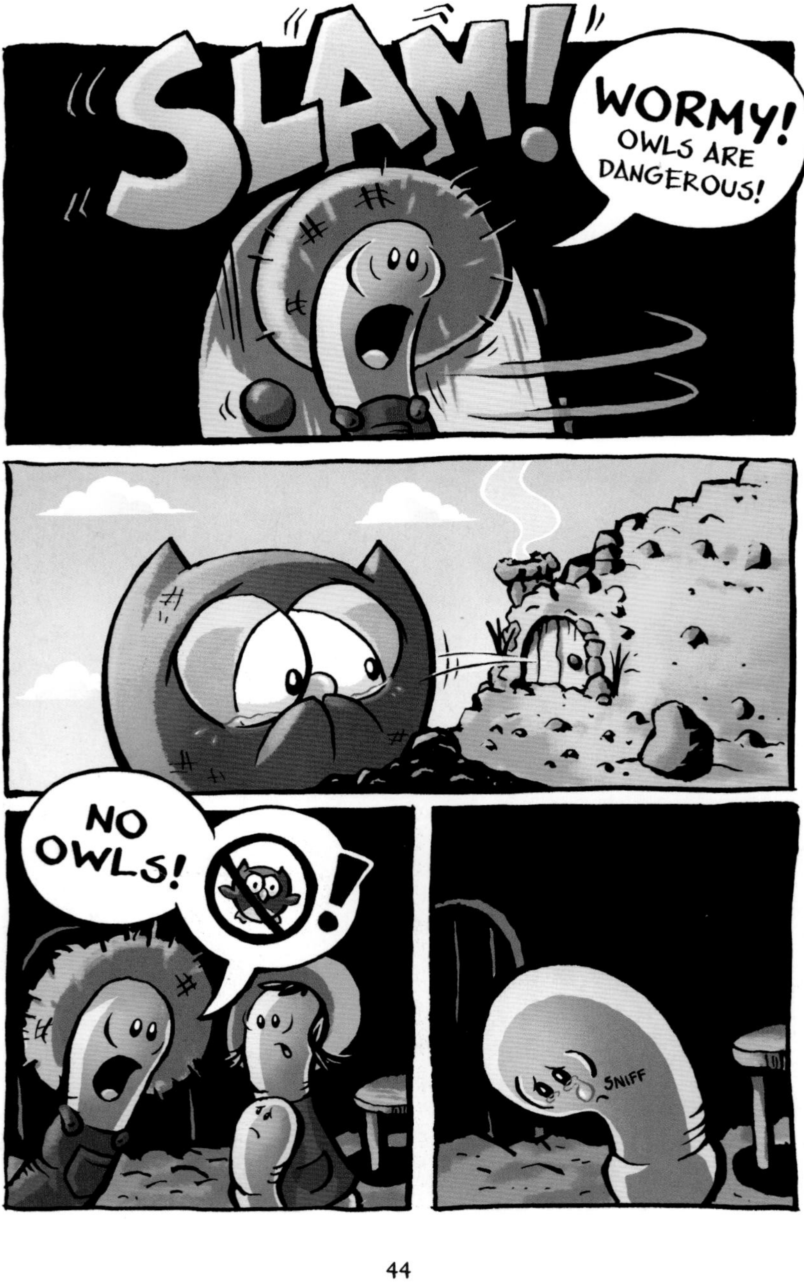
SLAM!
WORMY! OWLS ARE DANGEROUS!
NO OWLS!
!
SNIFF

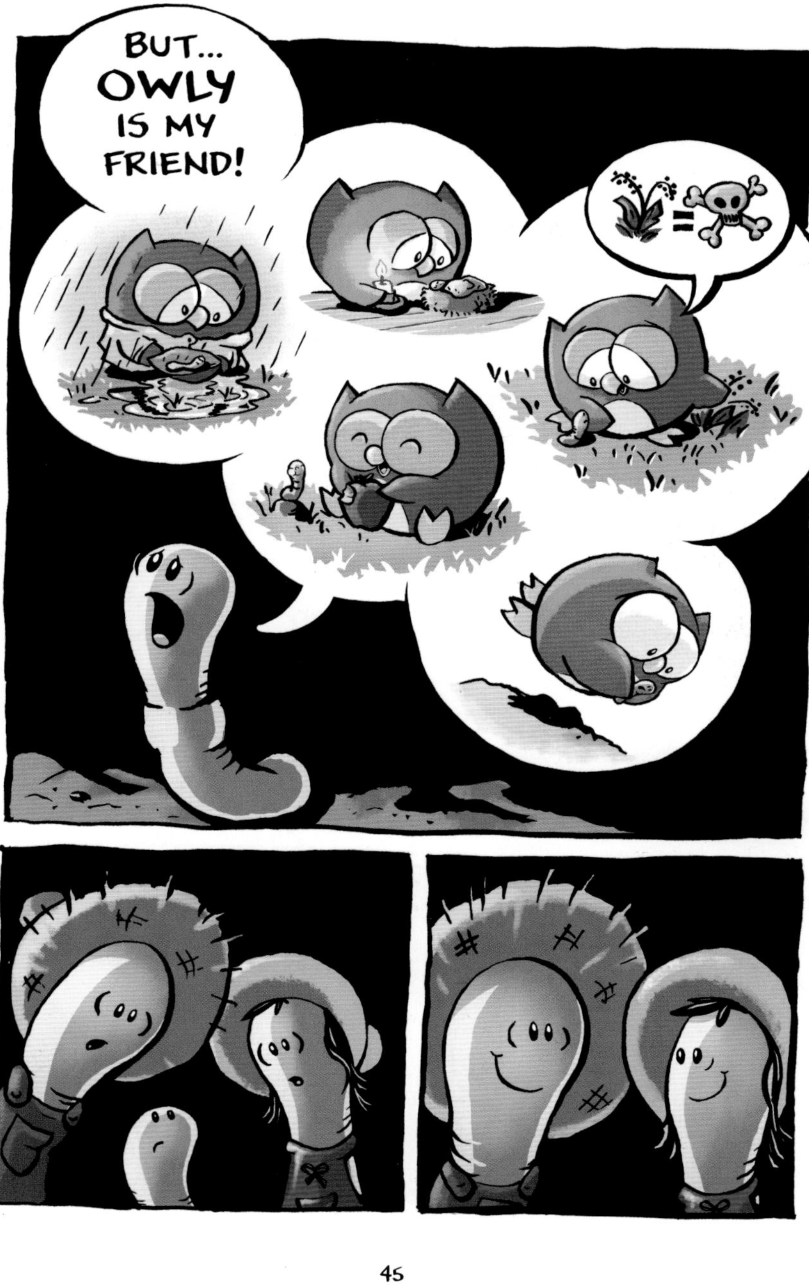
BUT... OWLY IS MY FRIEND!

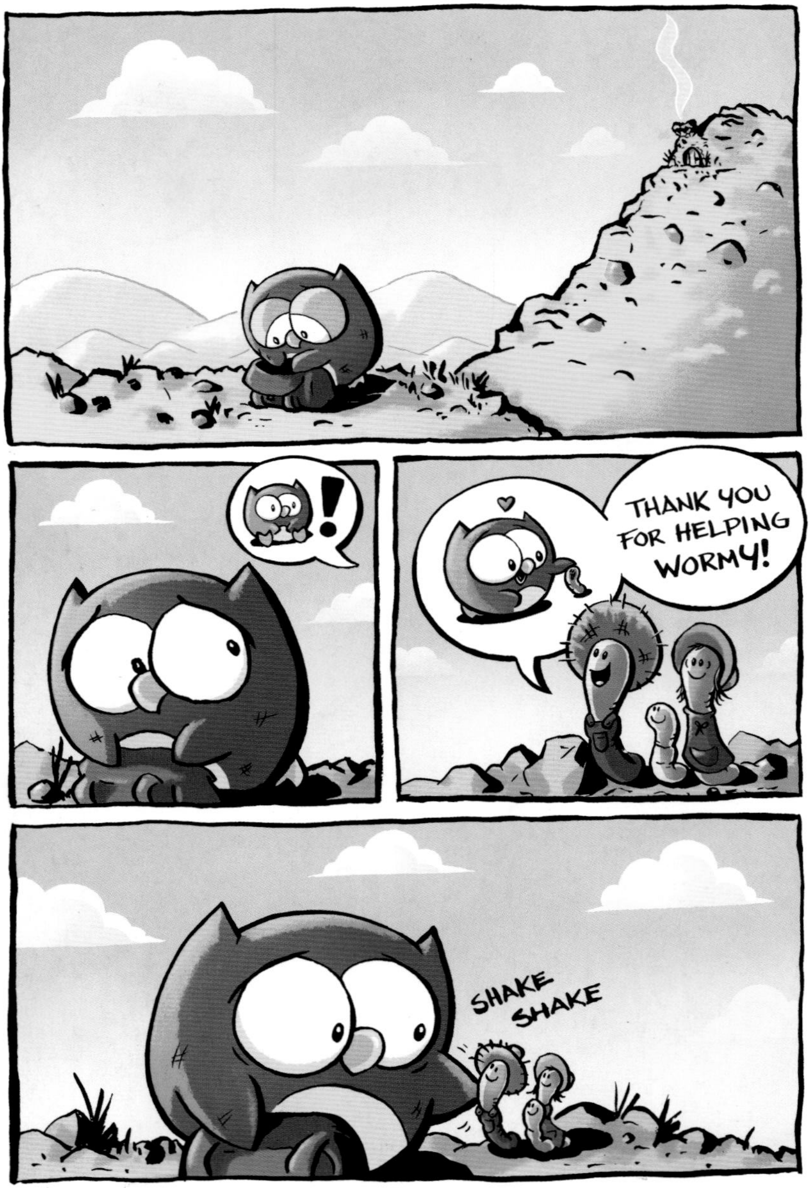
!
THANK YOU FOR HELPING WORMY!
SHAKE SHAKE

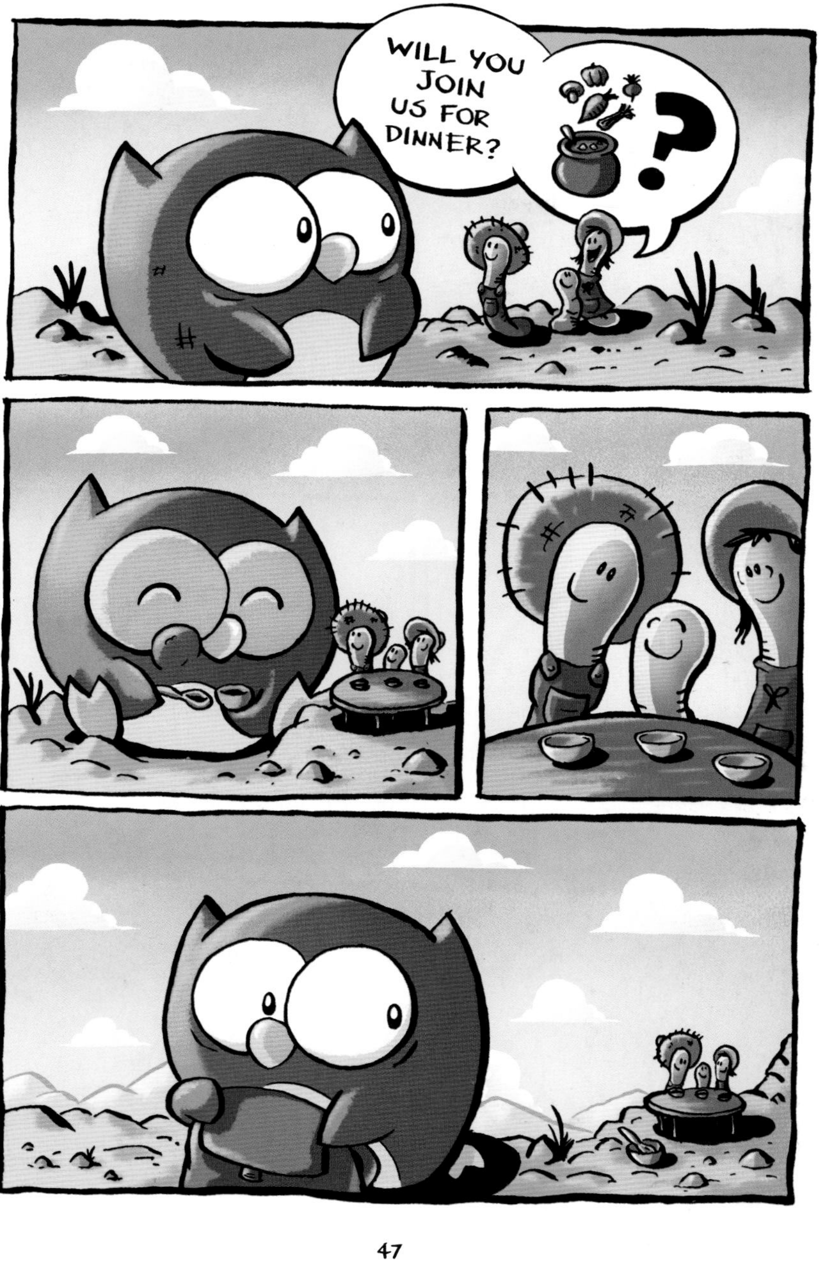
WILL YOU JOIN US FOR DINNER?
?

48

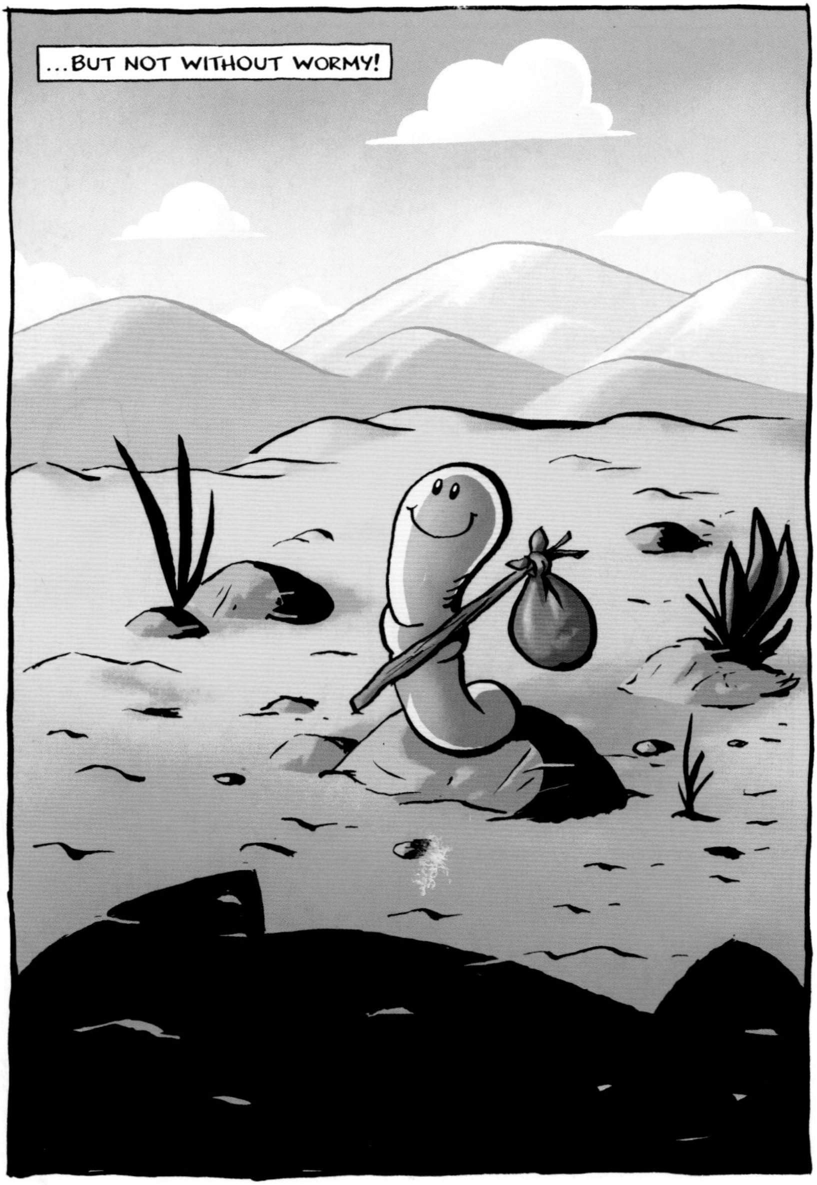
...BUT NOT WITHOUT WORMY!

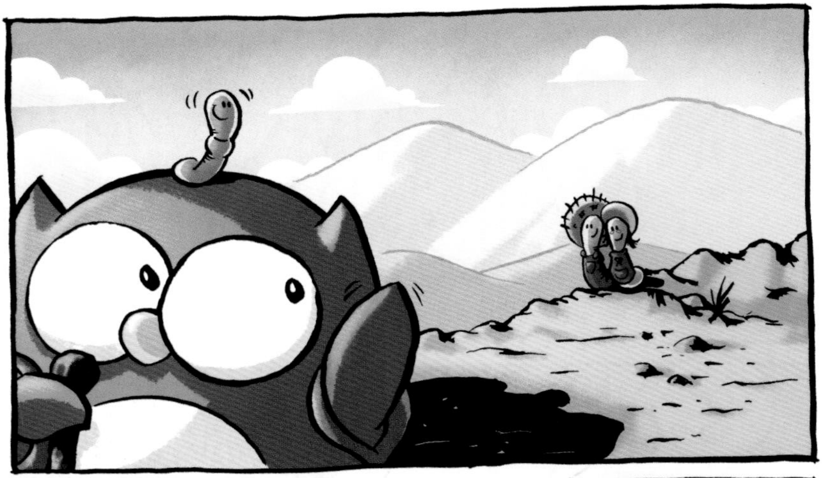

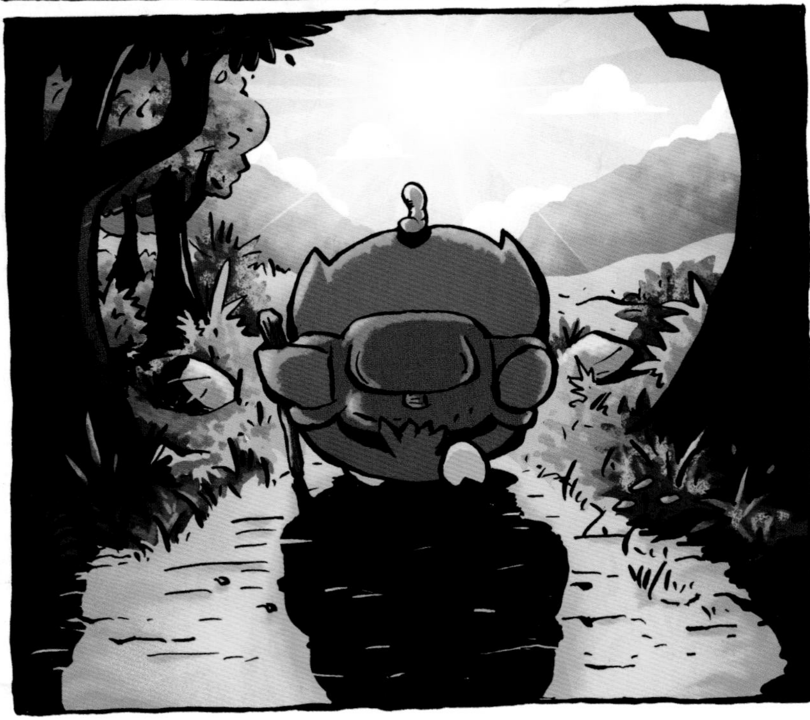

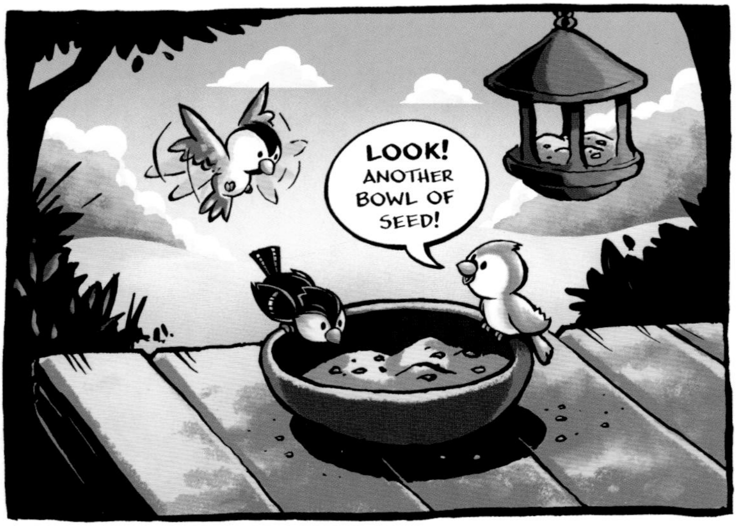
LOOK! ANOTHER BOWL OF SEED!

THE
END

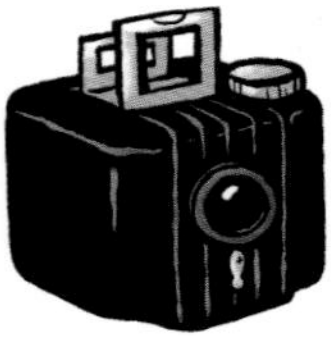

FLYING HOME

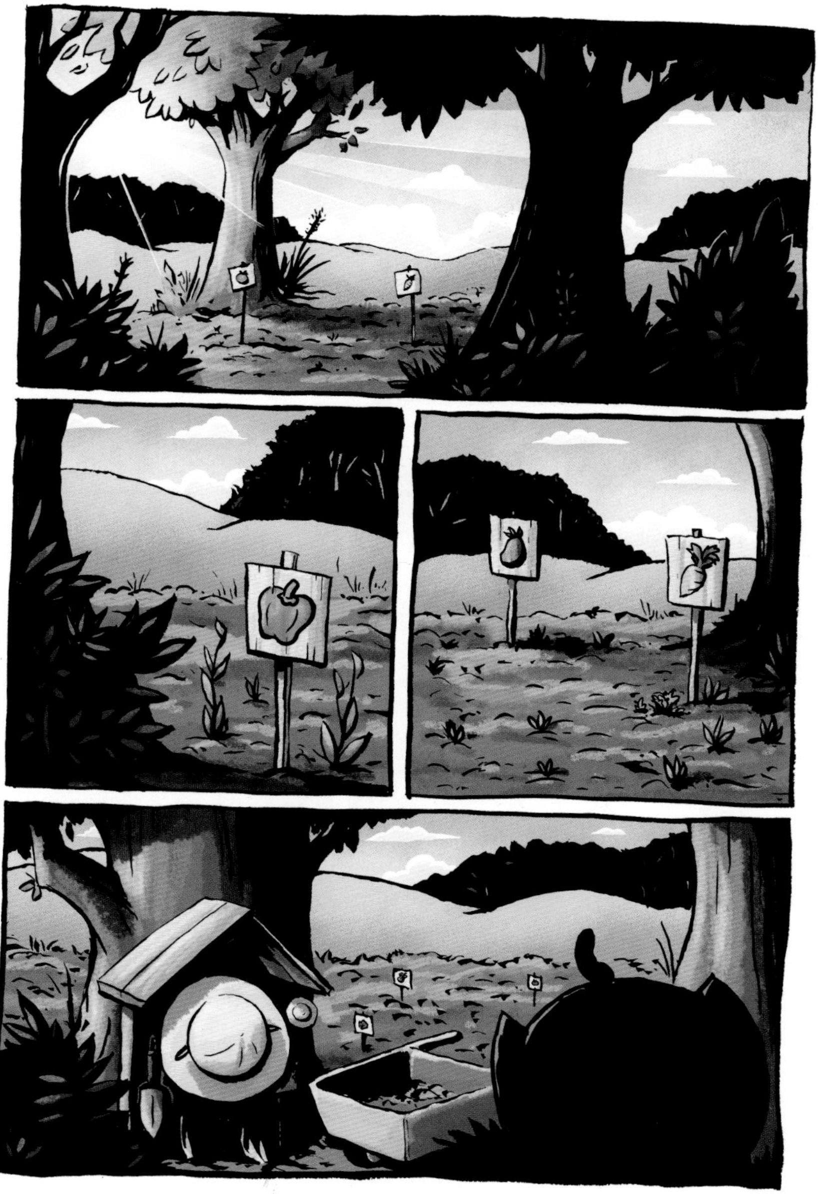

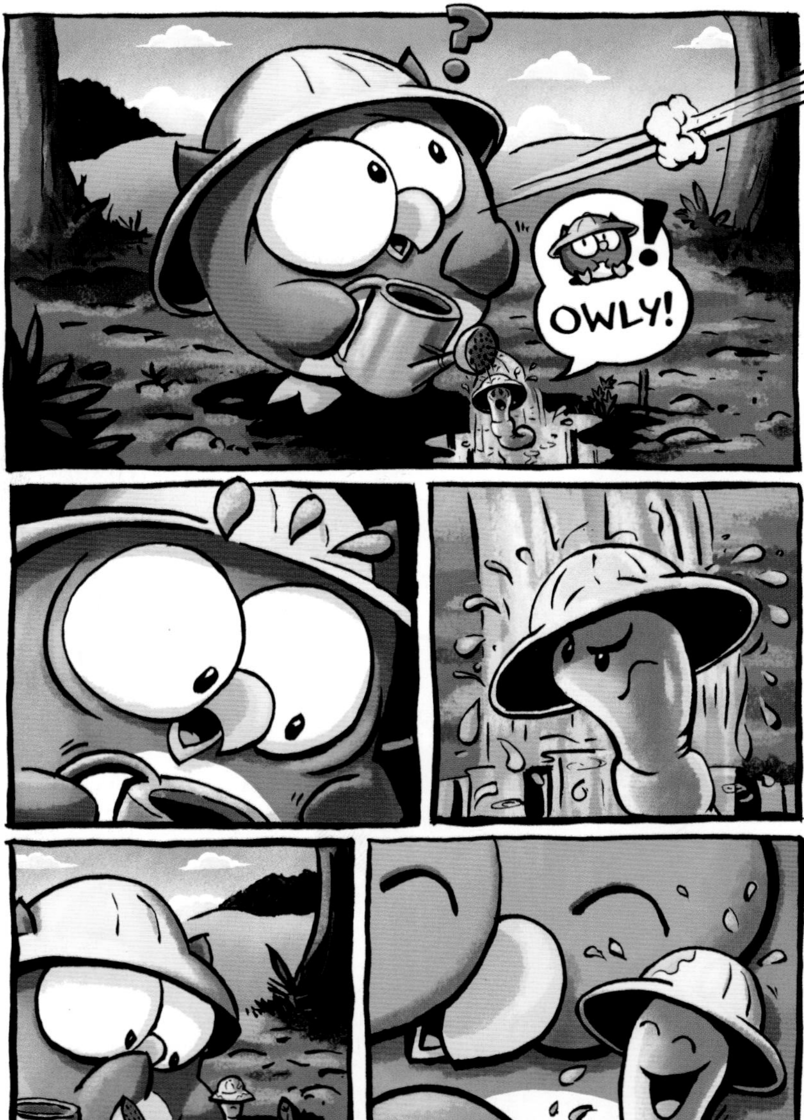
?
!
OWLY!

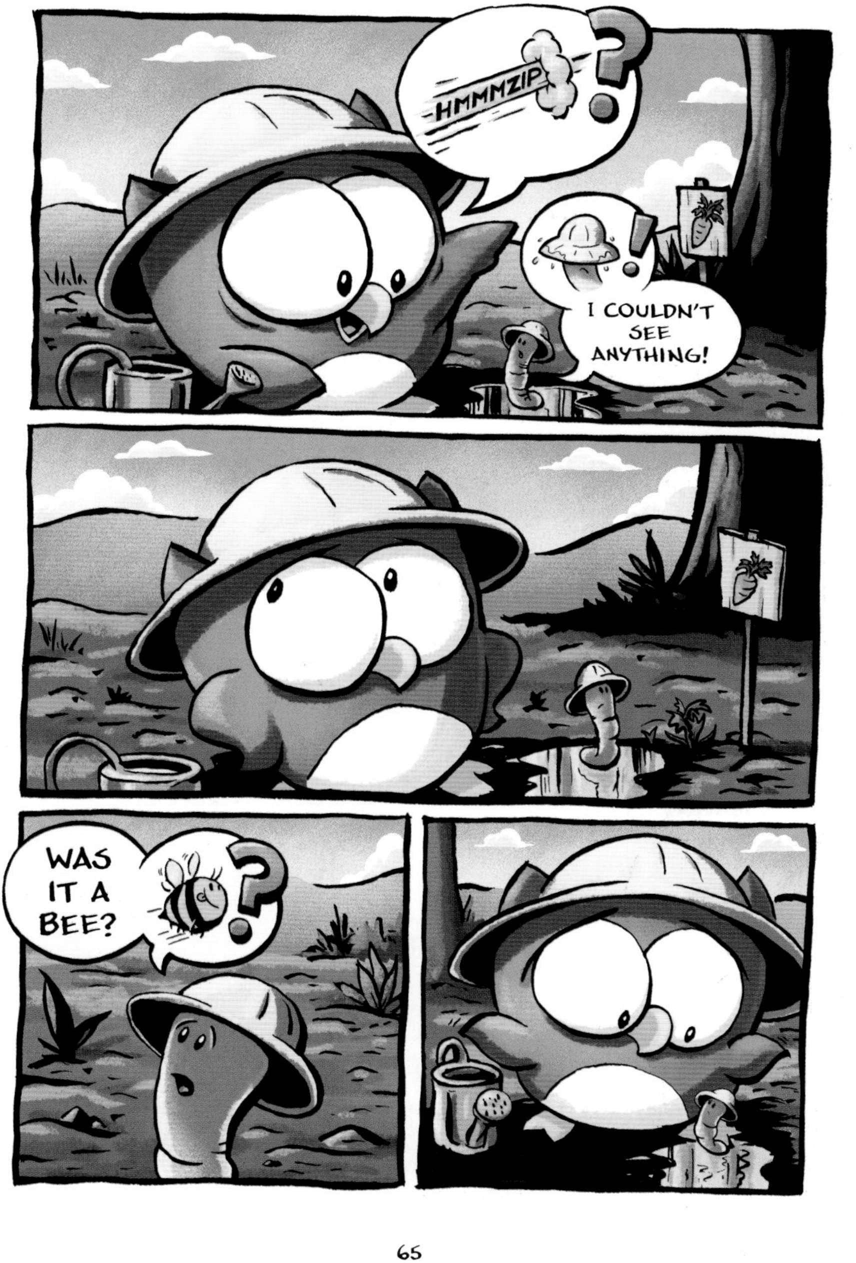
HMMMZIP
I COULDN'T SEE ANYTHING!
WAS IT A BEE?

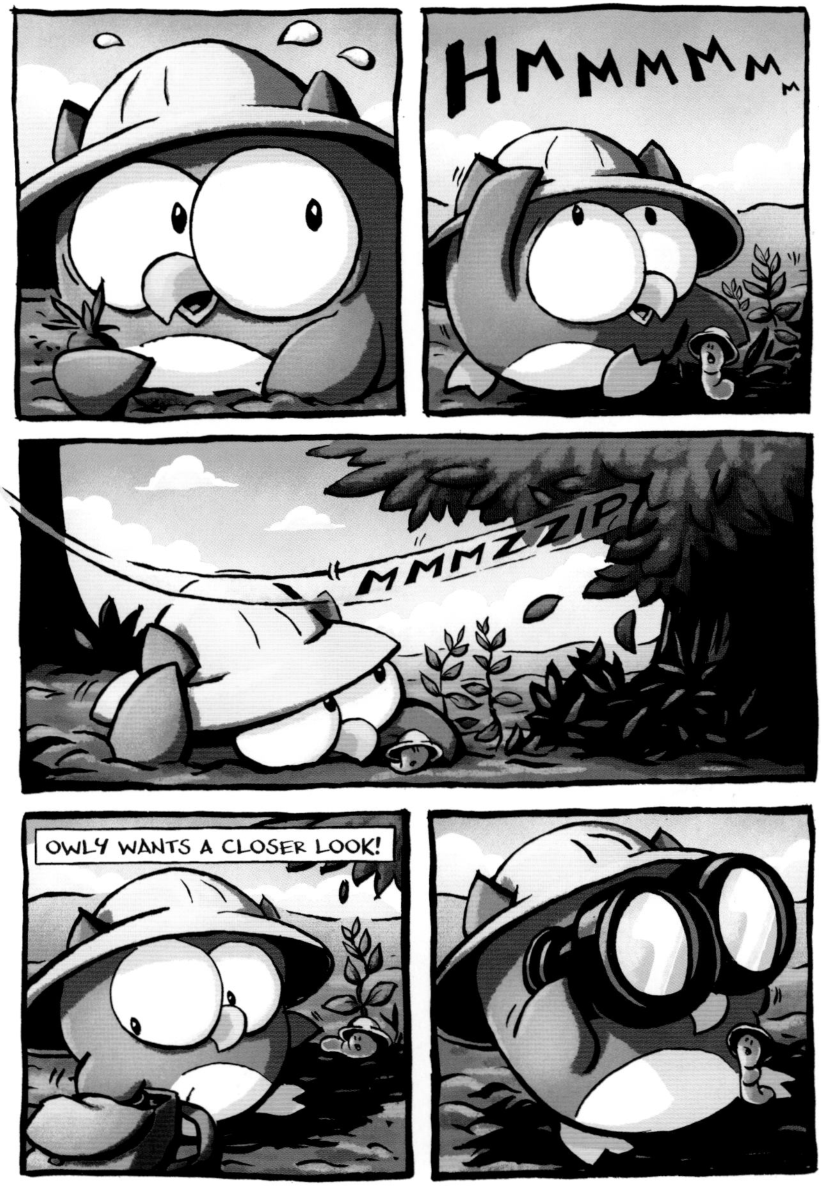
HMMMMMm
MMMZZZIP!
OWLY WANTS A CLOSER LOOK!

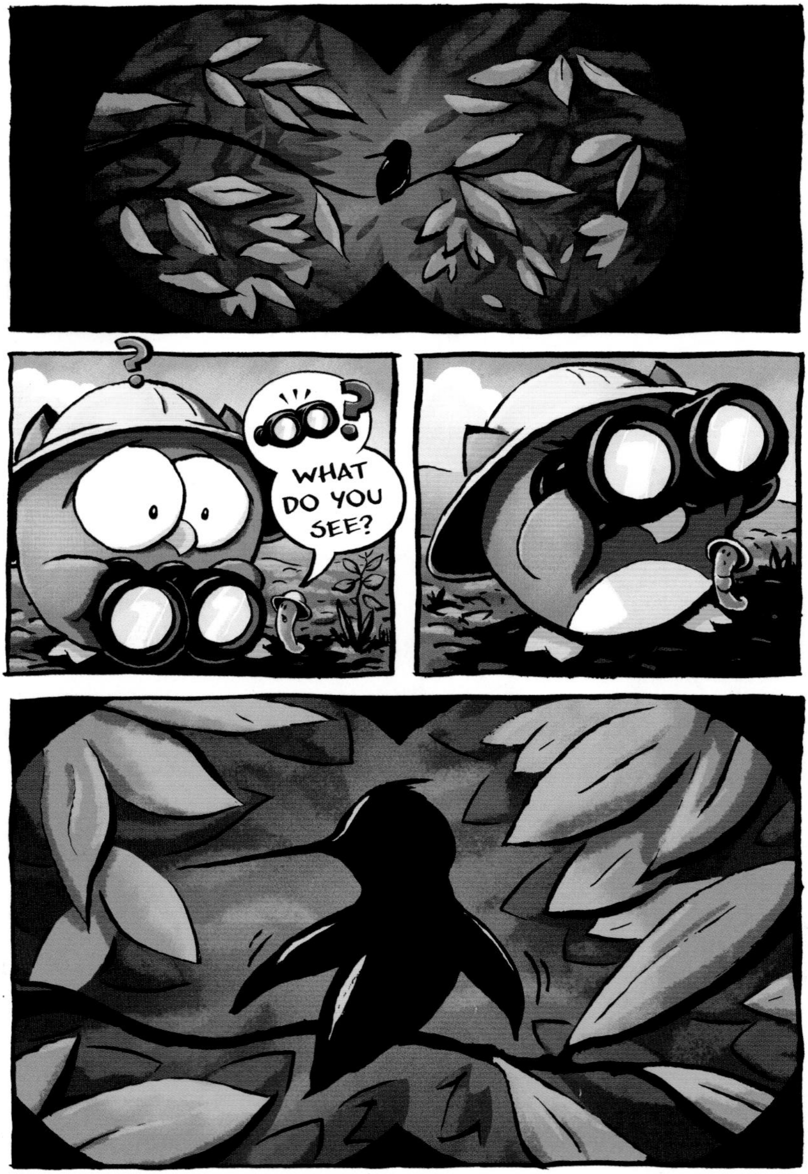
WHAT DO YOU SEE?

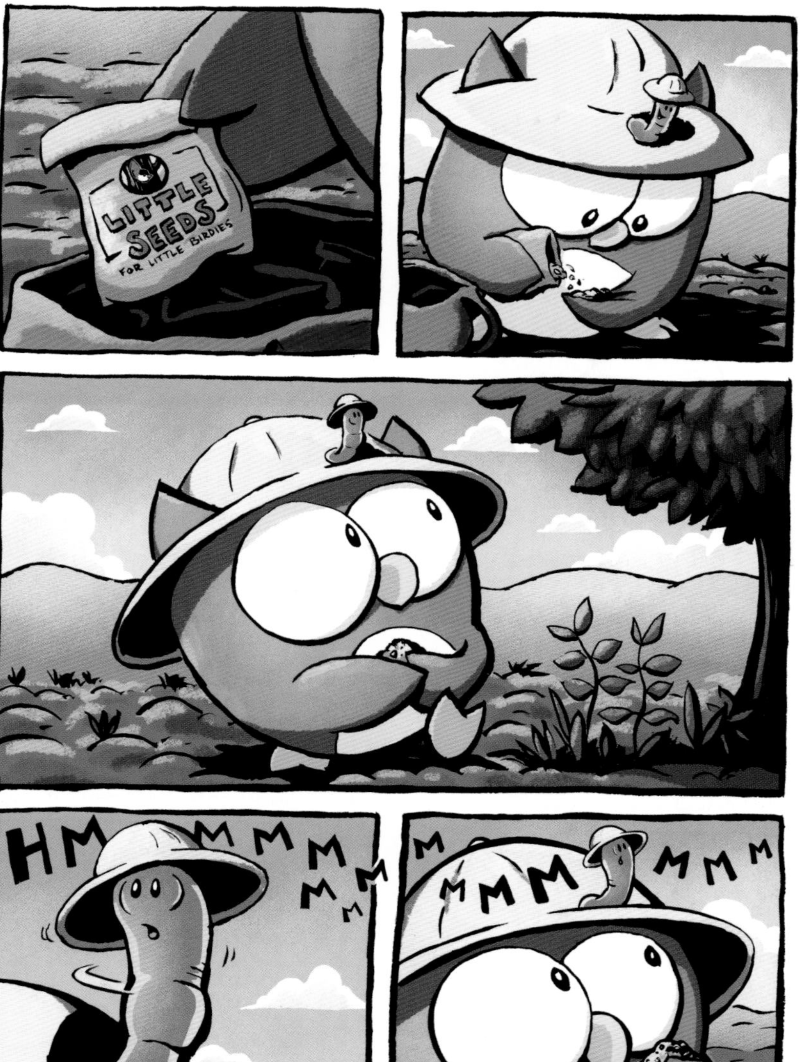
LITTLE SEEDS
FOR LITTLE BIRDIES
HMMMMMMMM
MMMMMMMM

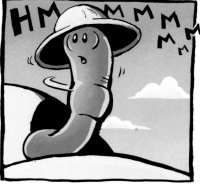

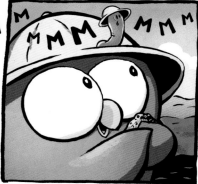

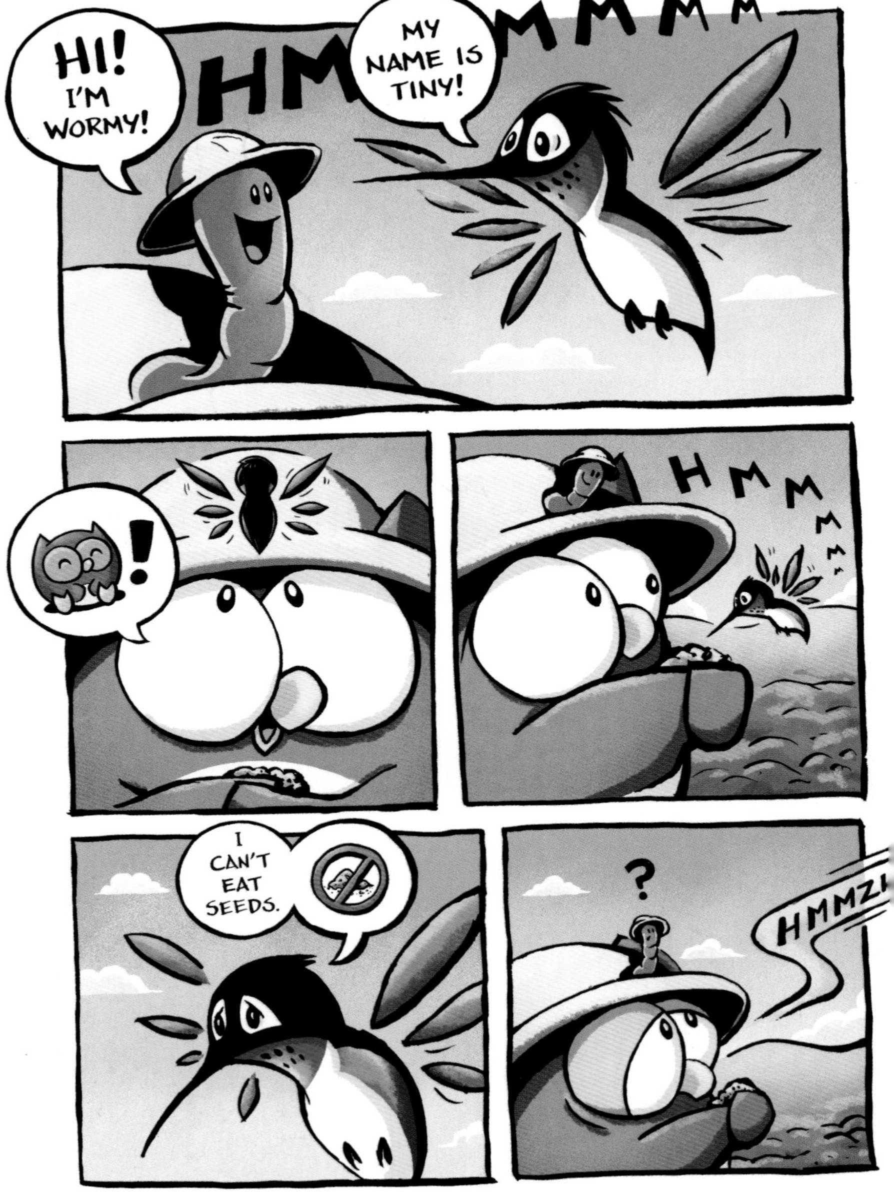
HI! I'M WORMY!
HMMMMMMM
MY NAME IS TINY!
!
HMMMMMM
I CAN'T EAT SEEDS.
?
HMMZI

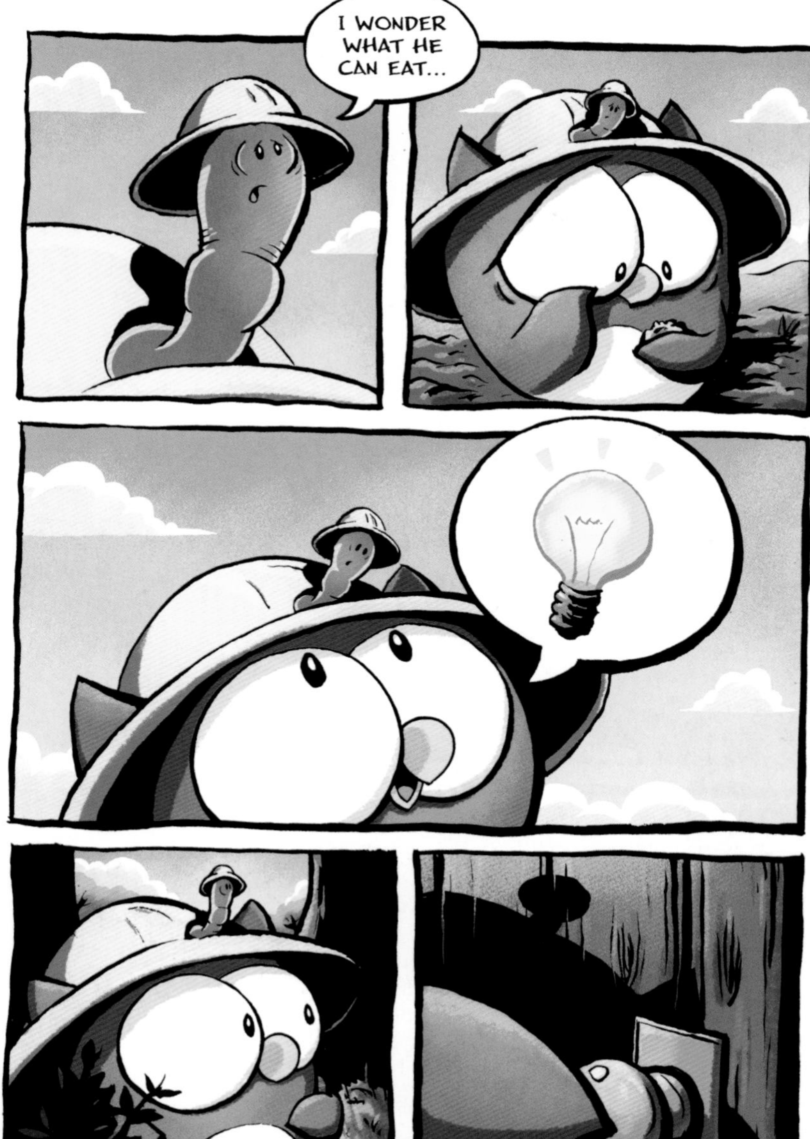
I WONDER WHAT HE CAN EAT...

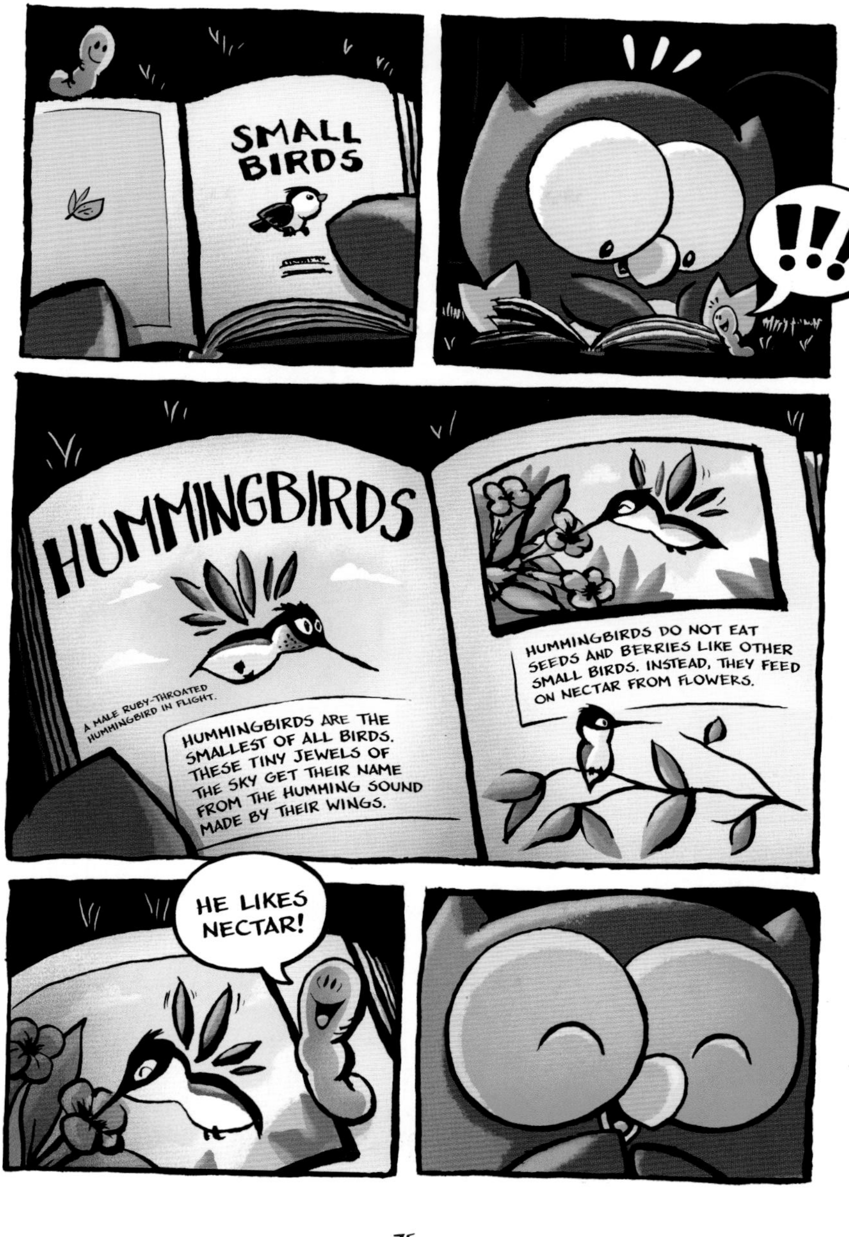
SMALL BIRDS
!!!
HUMMINGBIRDS
A MALE RUBY-THROATED HUMMINGBIRD IN FLIGHT.
HUMMINGBIRDS ARE THE SMALLEST OF ALL BIRDS. THESE TINY JEWELS OF THE SKY GET THEIR NAME FROM THE HUMMING SOUND MADE BY THEIR WINGS.
HUMMINGBIRDS DO NOT EAT SEEDS AND BERRIES LIKE OTHER SMALL BIRDS. INSTEAD, THEY FEED ON NECTAR FROM FLOWERS.
HE LIKES NECTAR!

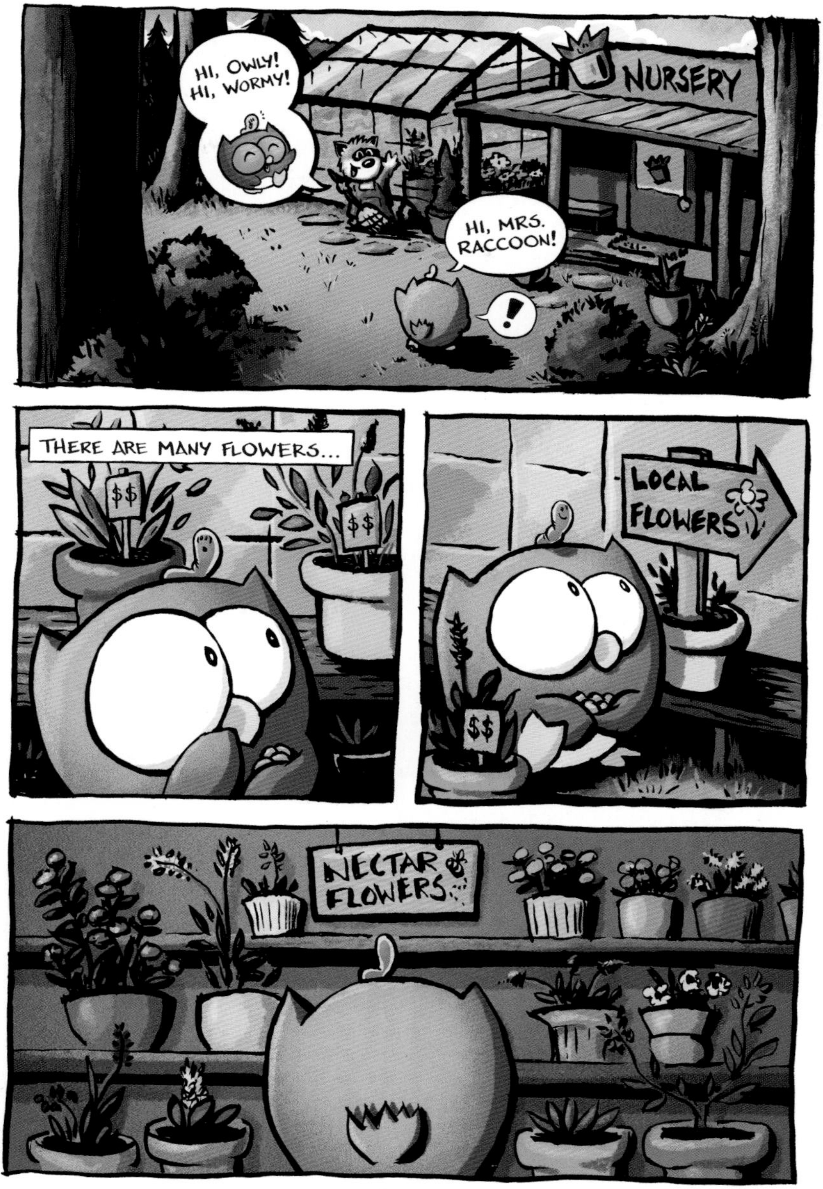

HI, OWLY! HI, WORMY!
NURSERY
HI, MRS. RACCOON!
!
THERE ARE MANY FLOWERS...
$$
$$
LOCAL FLOWERS
$$
NECTAR FLOWERS

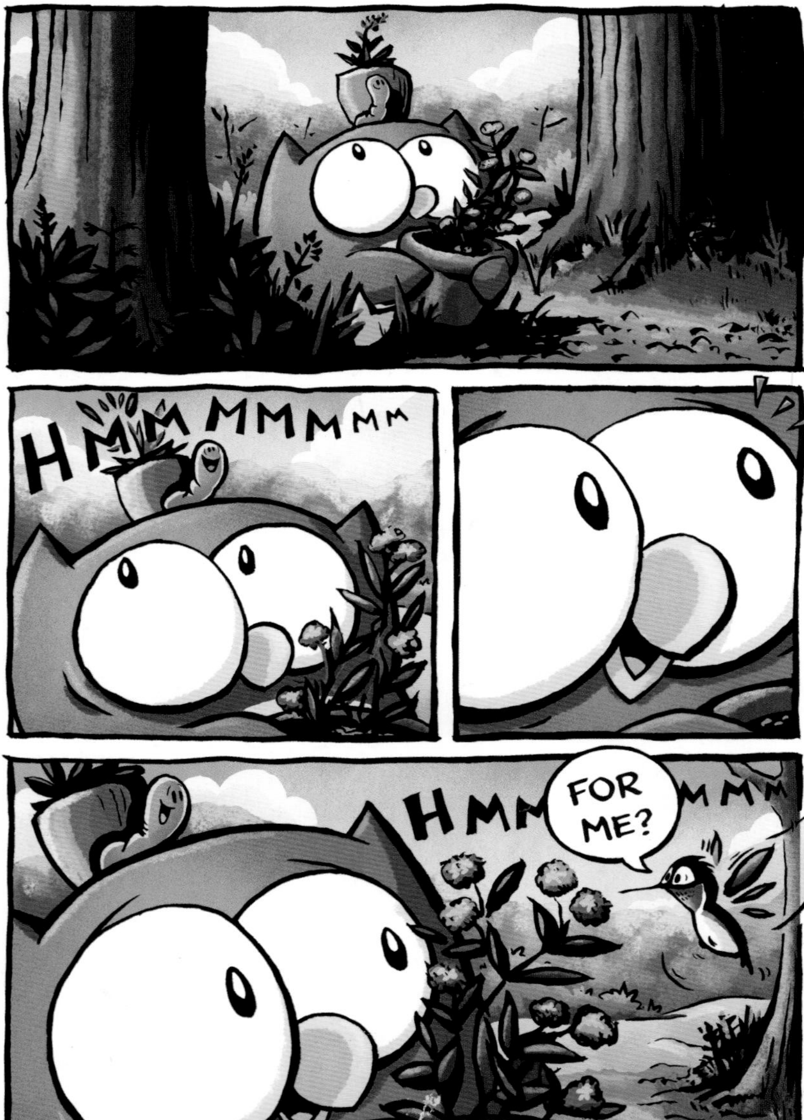
HMMMMMMM
HMM
FOR ME?
MMM

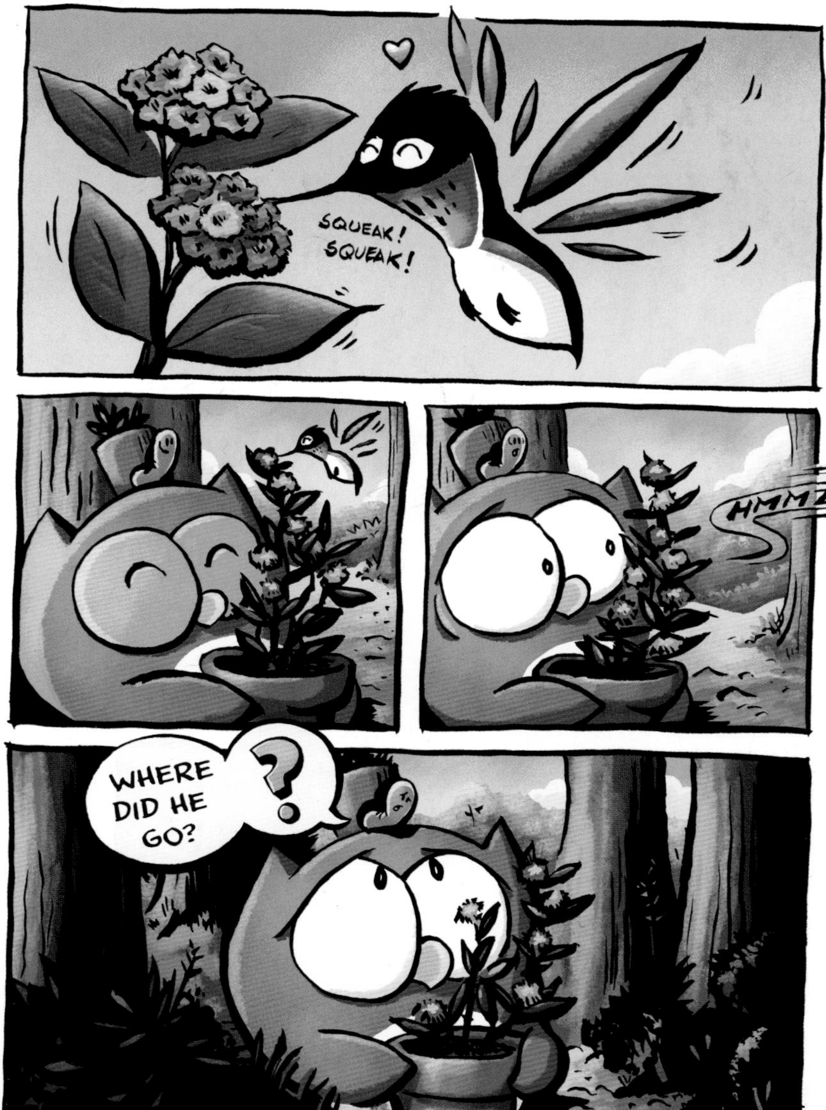
SQUEAK! SQUEAK!
HMMZIP
WHERE DID HE GO?
?

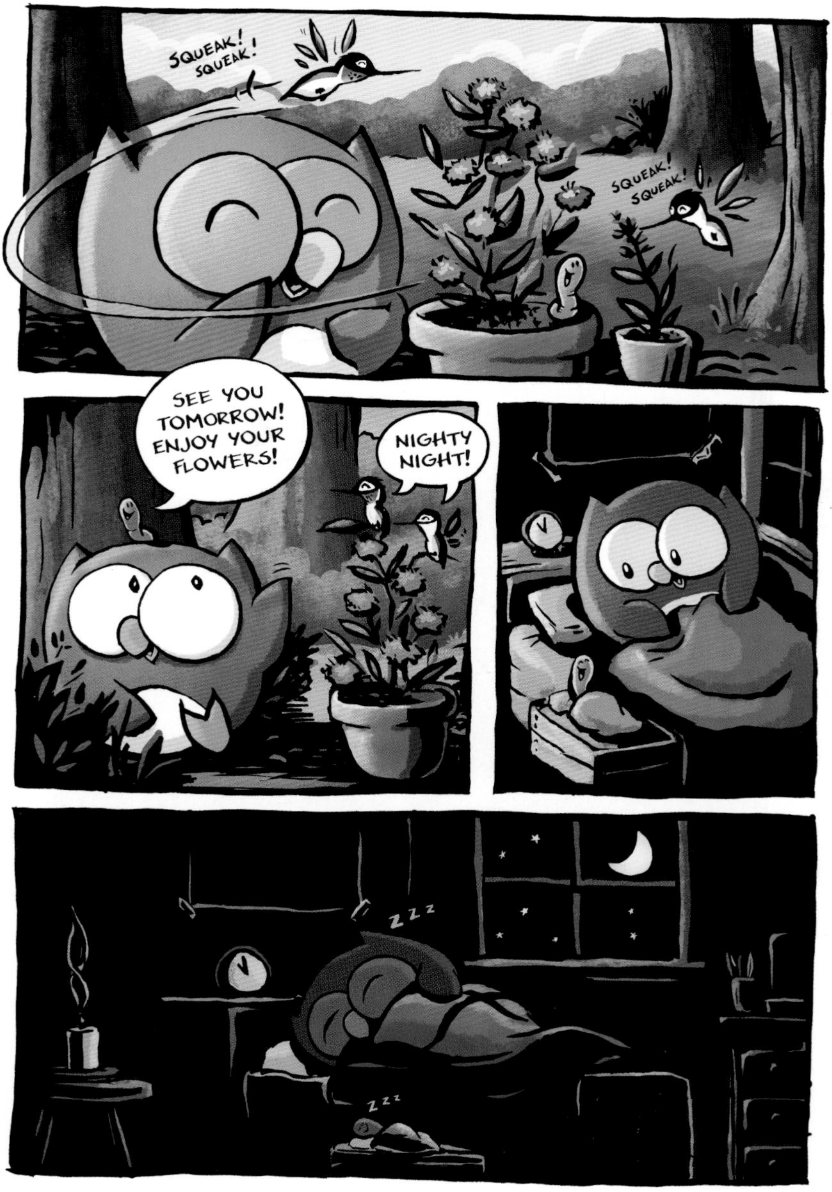
SQUEAK! SQUEAK!
SQUEAK! SQUEAK!
SEE YOU TOMORROW! ENJOY YOUR FLOWERS!
NIGHTY NIGHT!
Z Z Z
Z Z Z

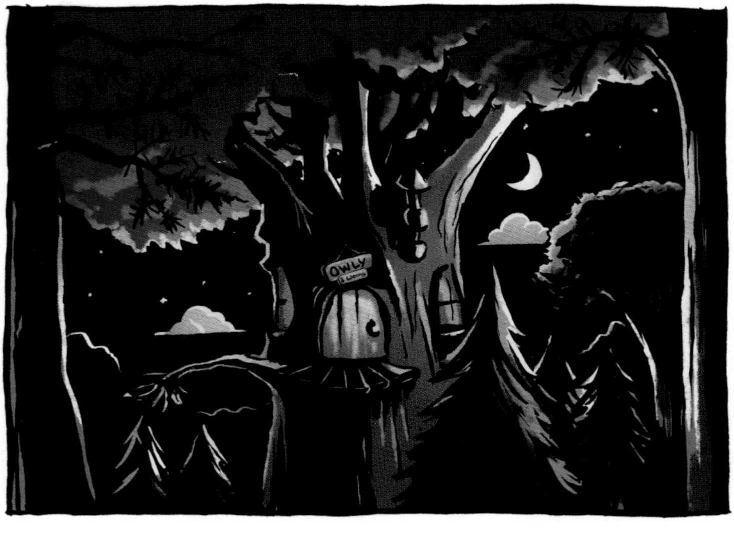
OWLY

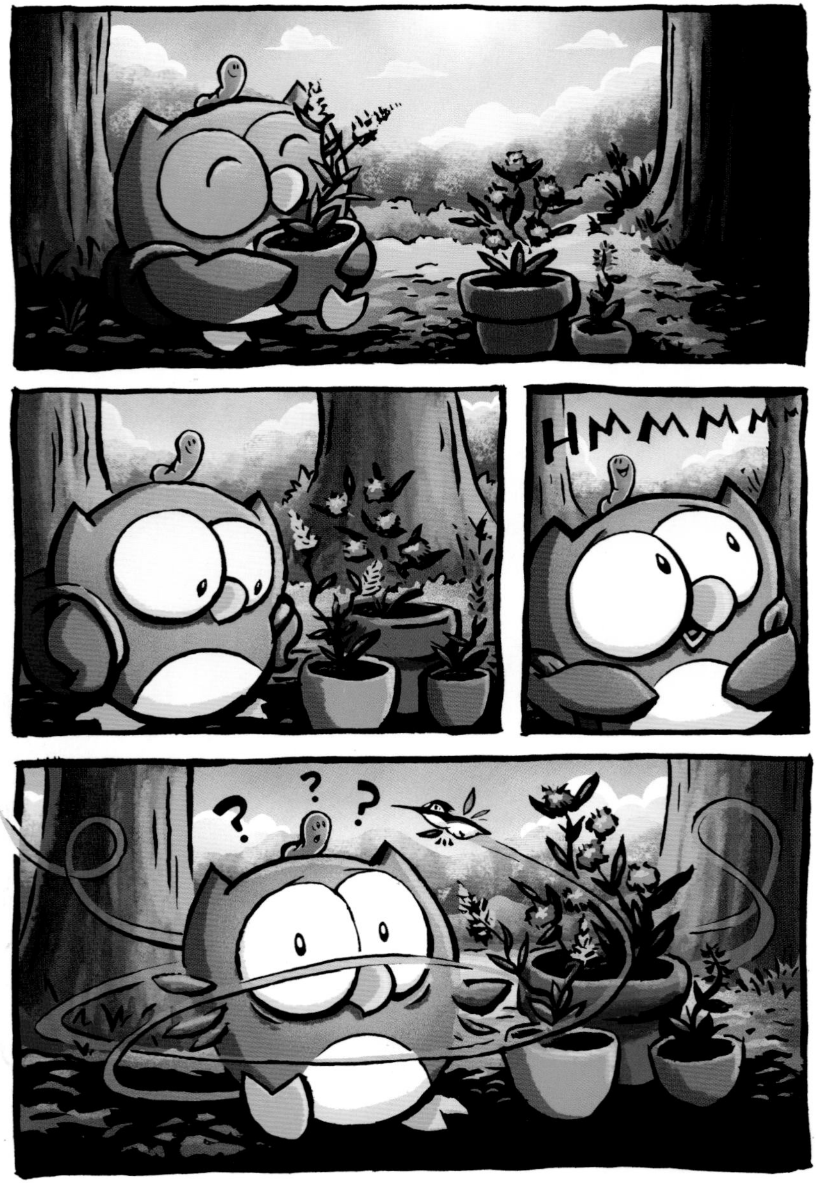
HMMMM
? ? ?

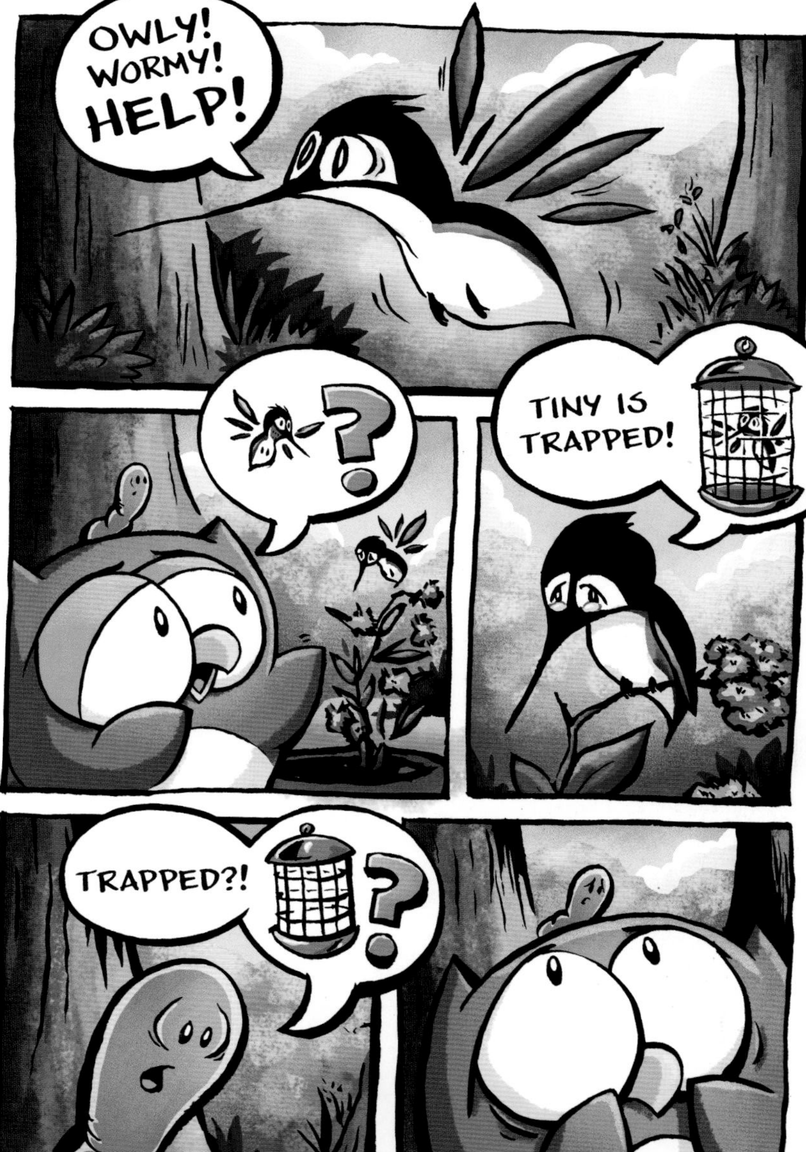
OWLY! WORMY! HELP!
TINY IS TRAPPED!
TRAPPED?!

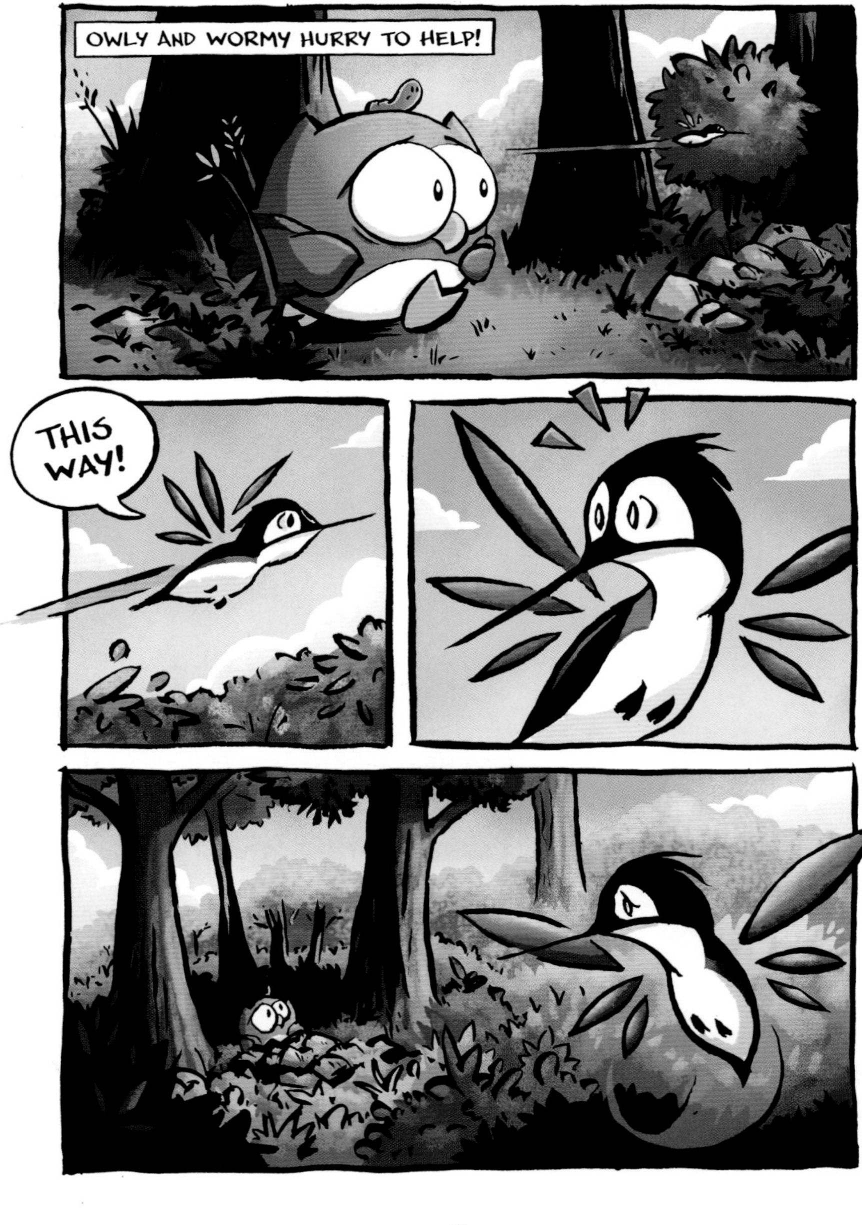
OWLY AND WORMY HURRY TO HELP!
THIS WAY!

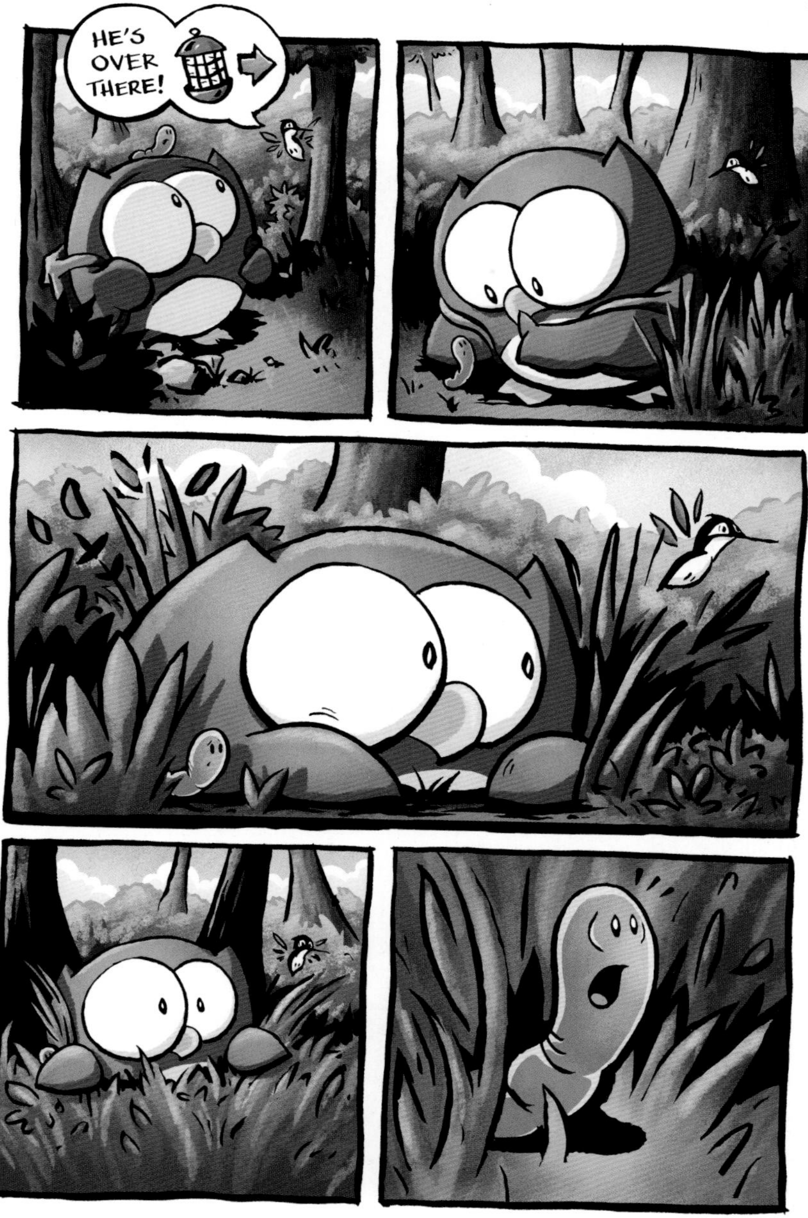
HE'S OVER THERE!

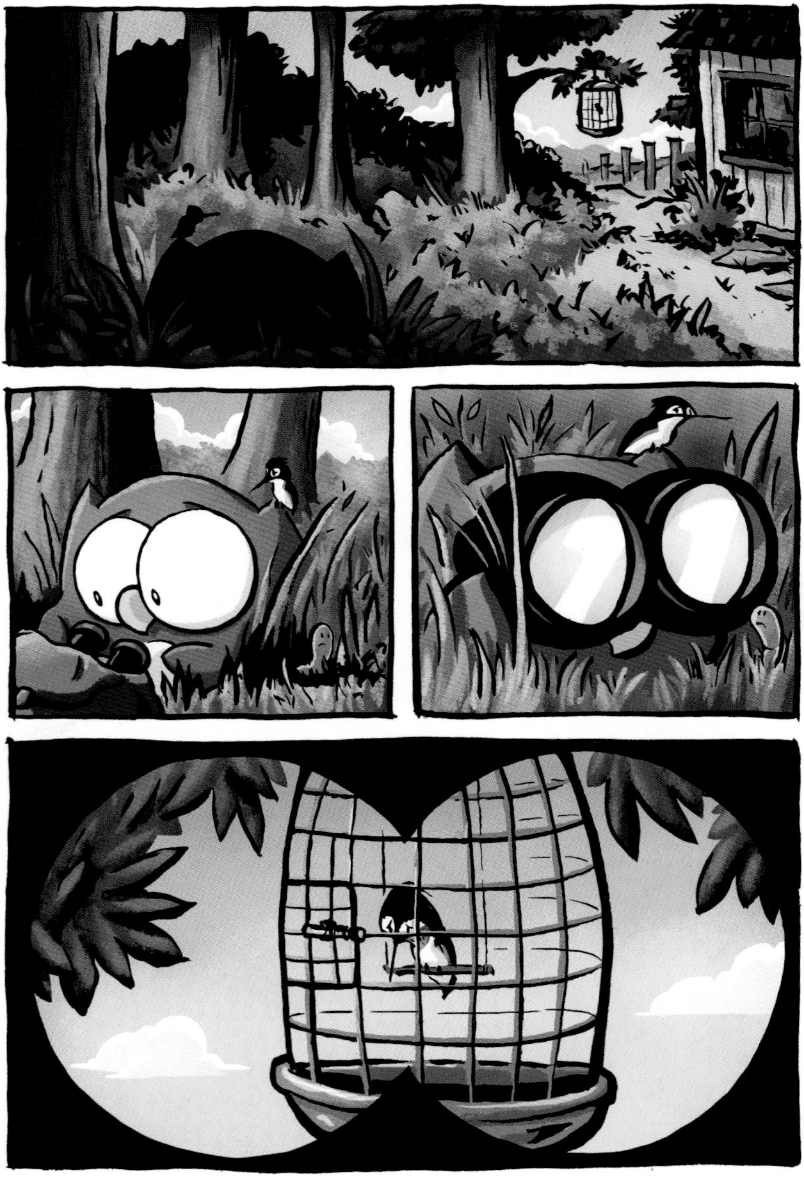

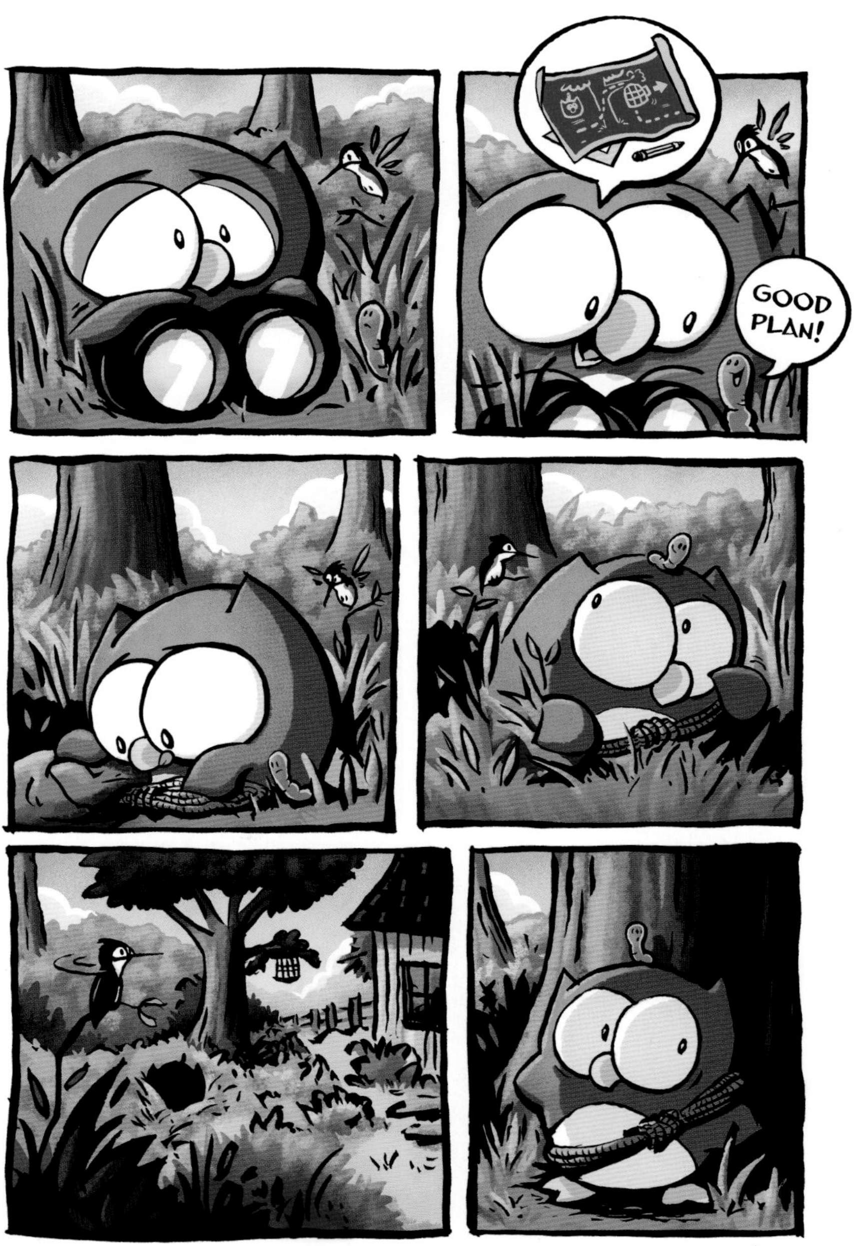
GOOD PLAN!

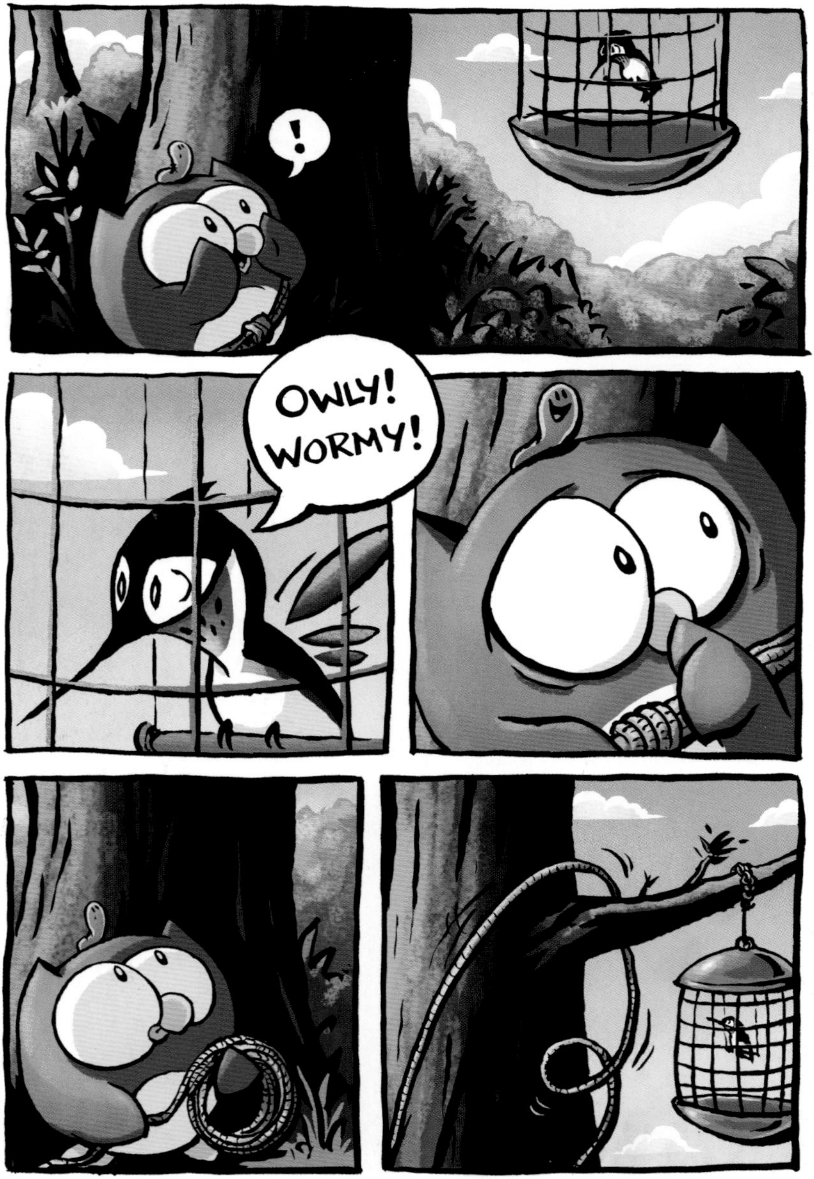
!
OWLY! WORMY!

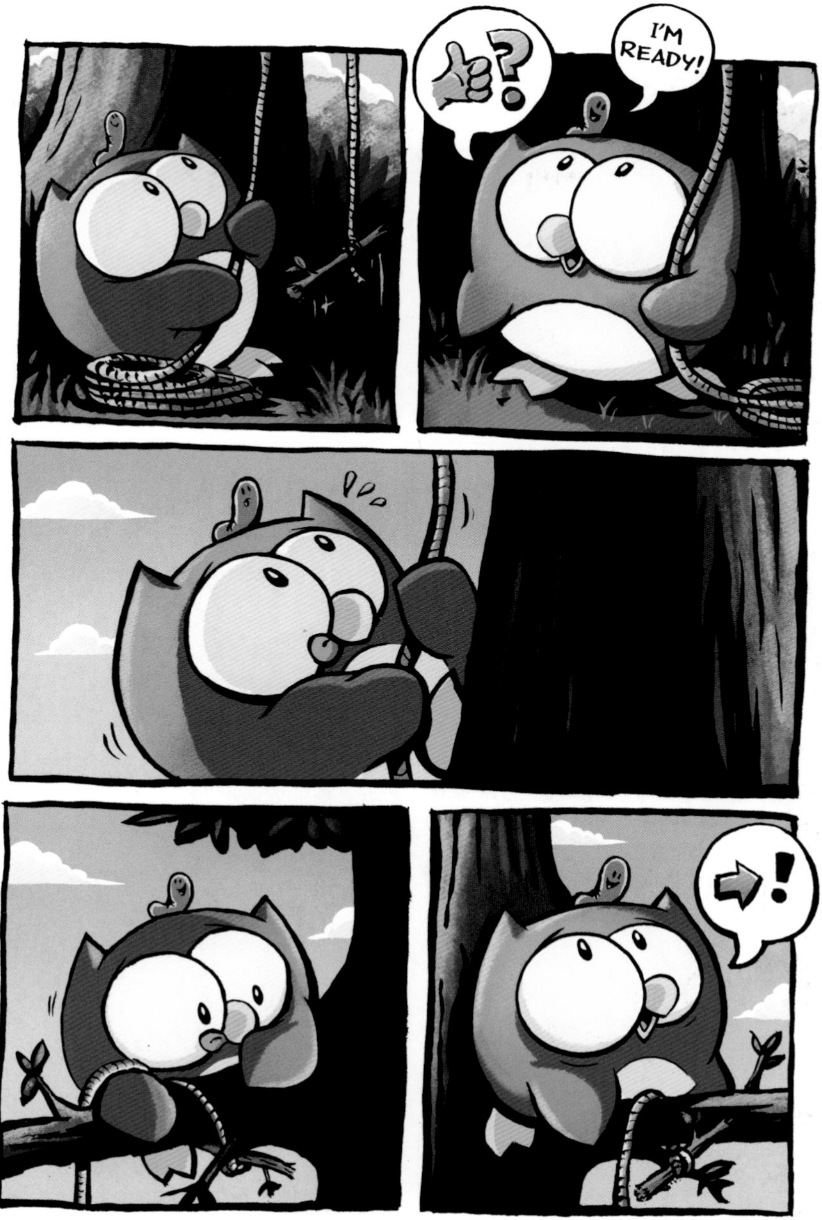
I'M READY!

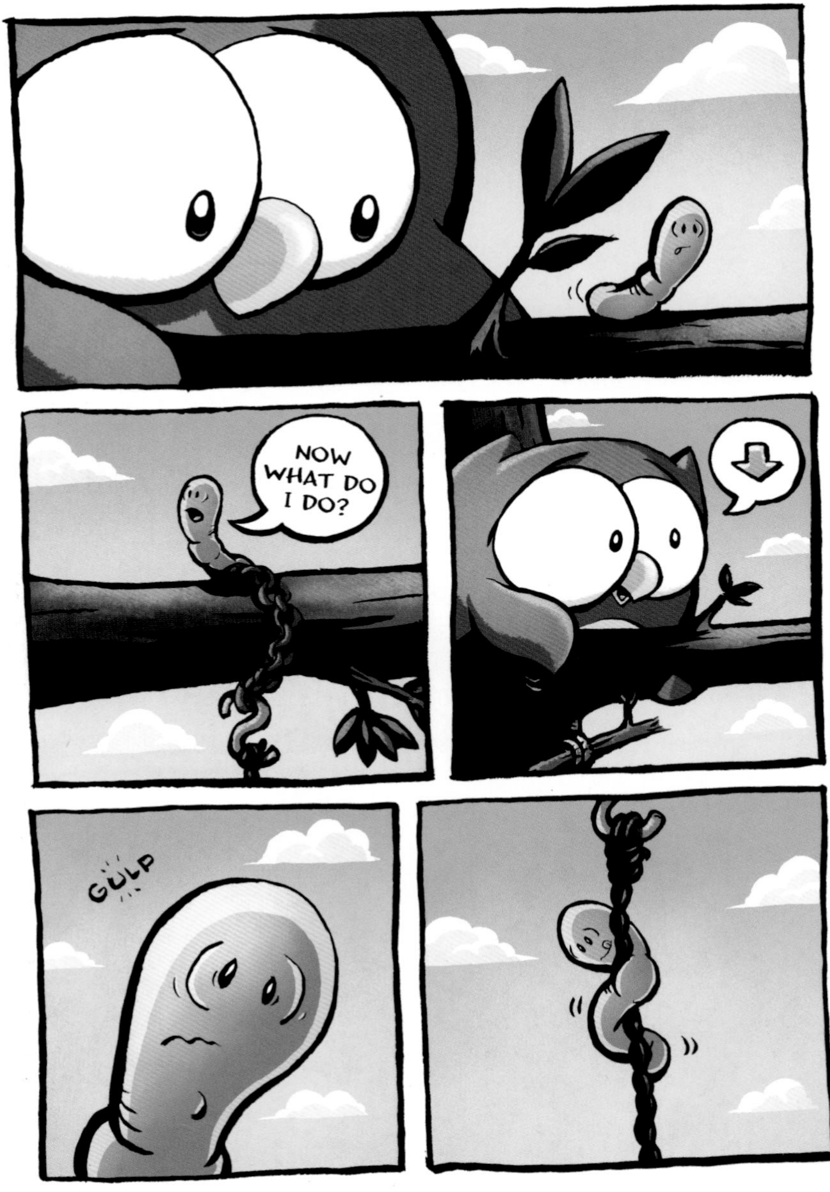
NOW WHAT DO I DO?
GULP

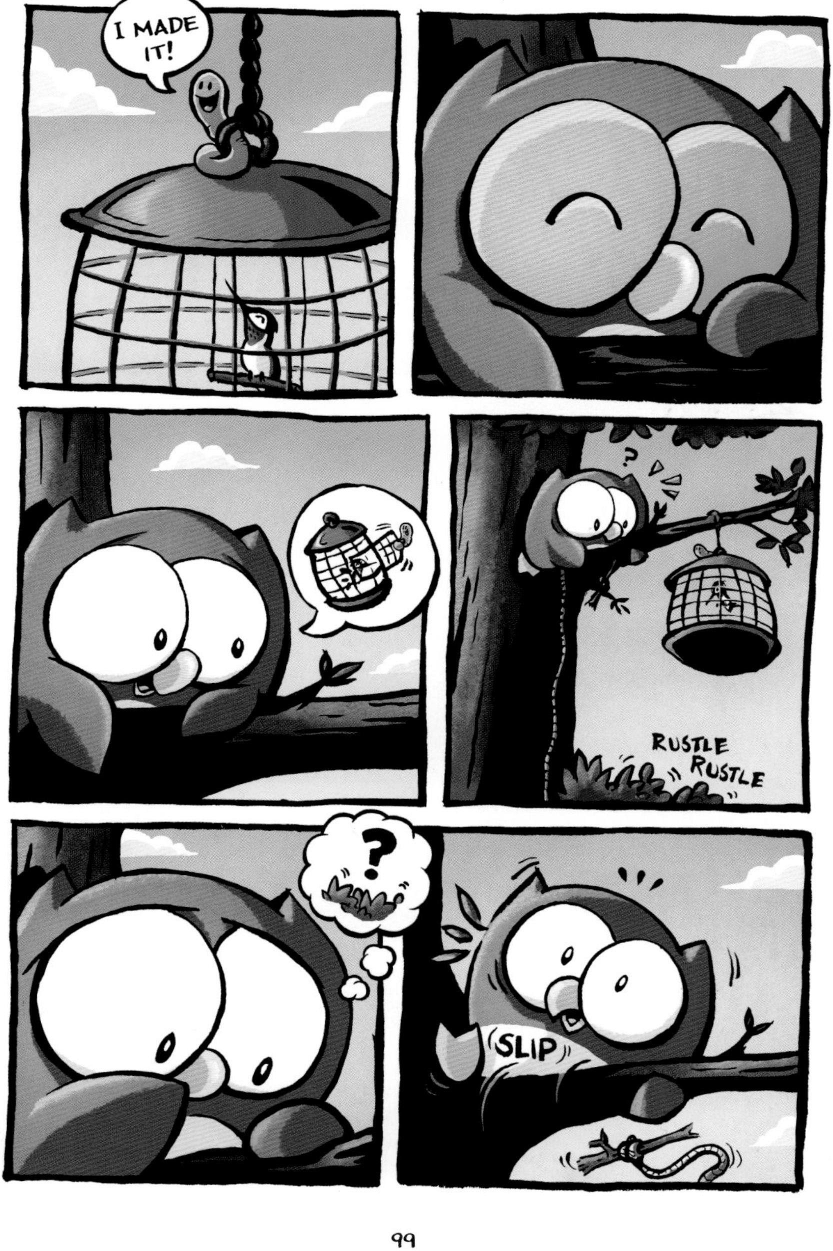
I MADE IT!
?
RUSTLE RUSTLE
?
SLIP

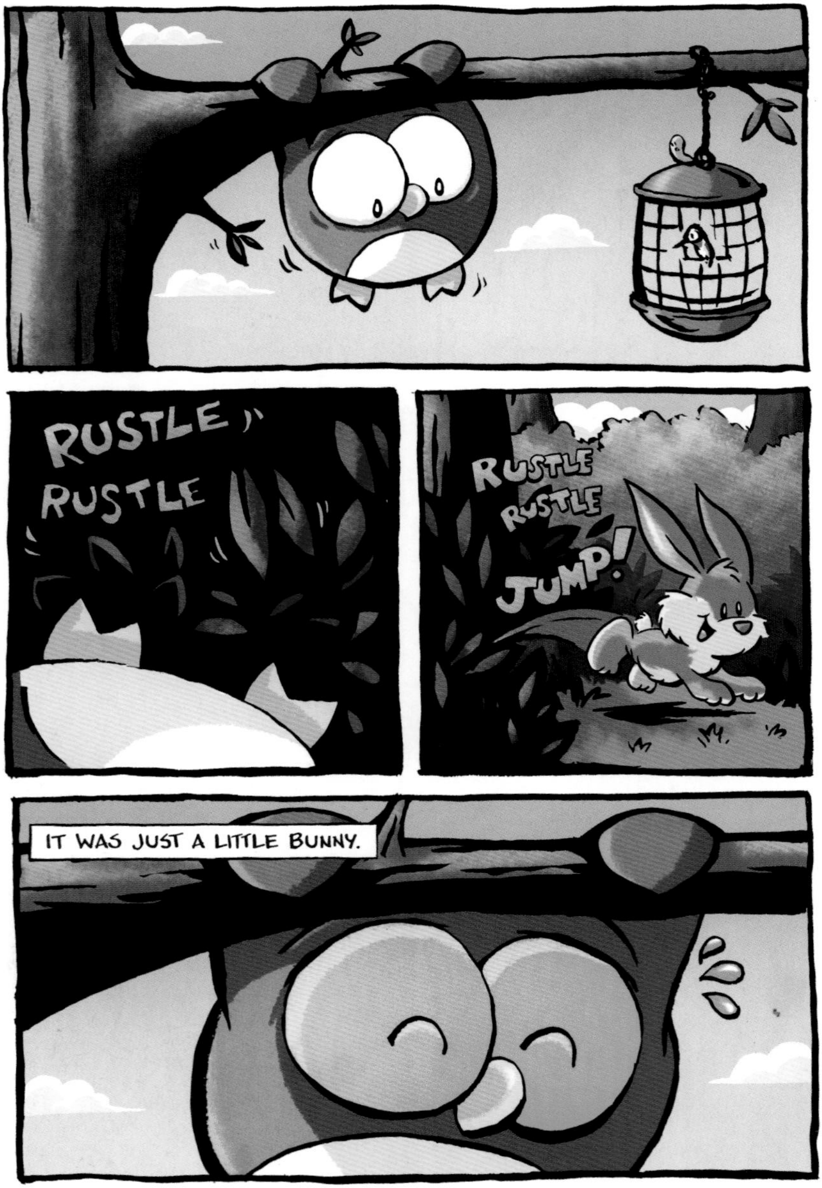
RUSTLE
RUSTLE
RUSTLE
RUSTLE
JUMP!
IT WAS JUST A LITTLE BUNNY.

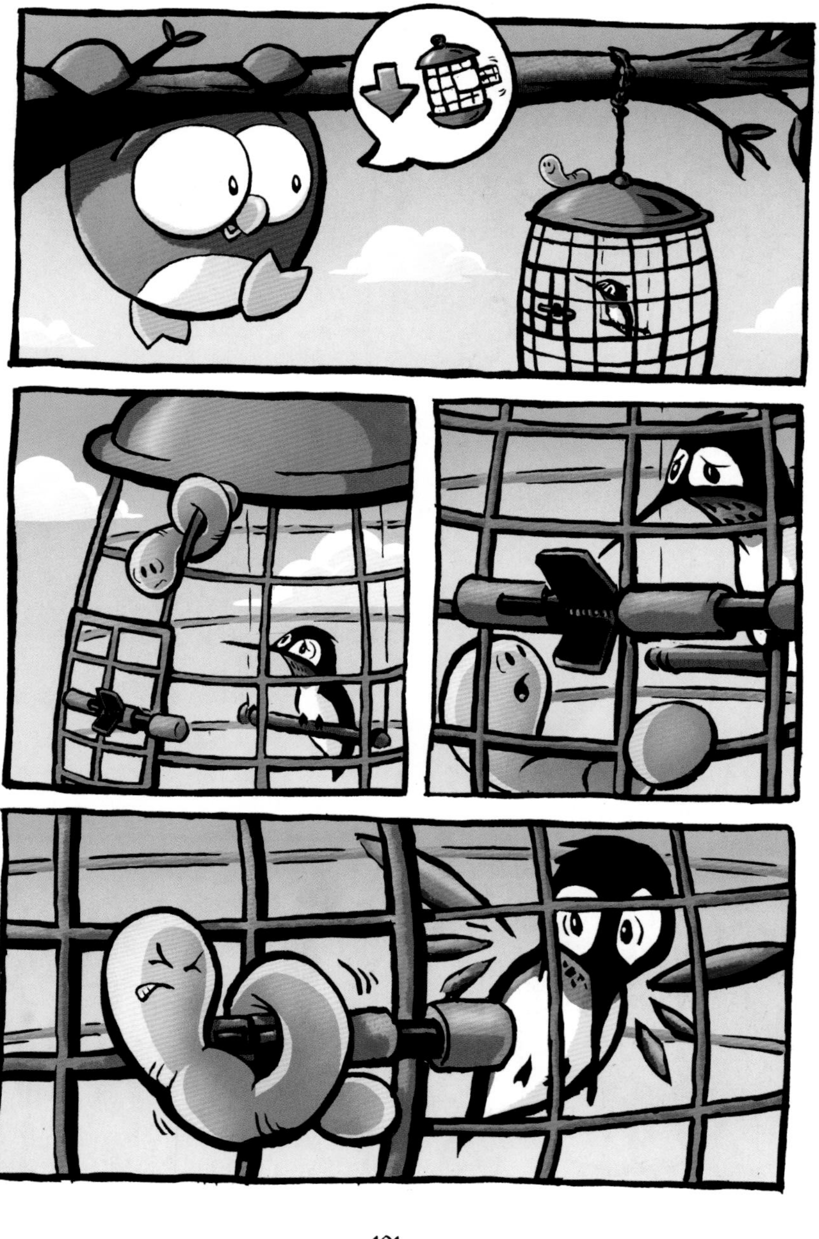

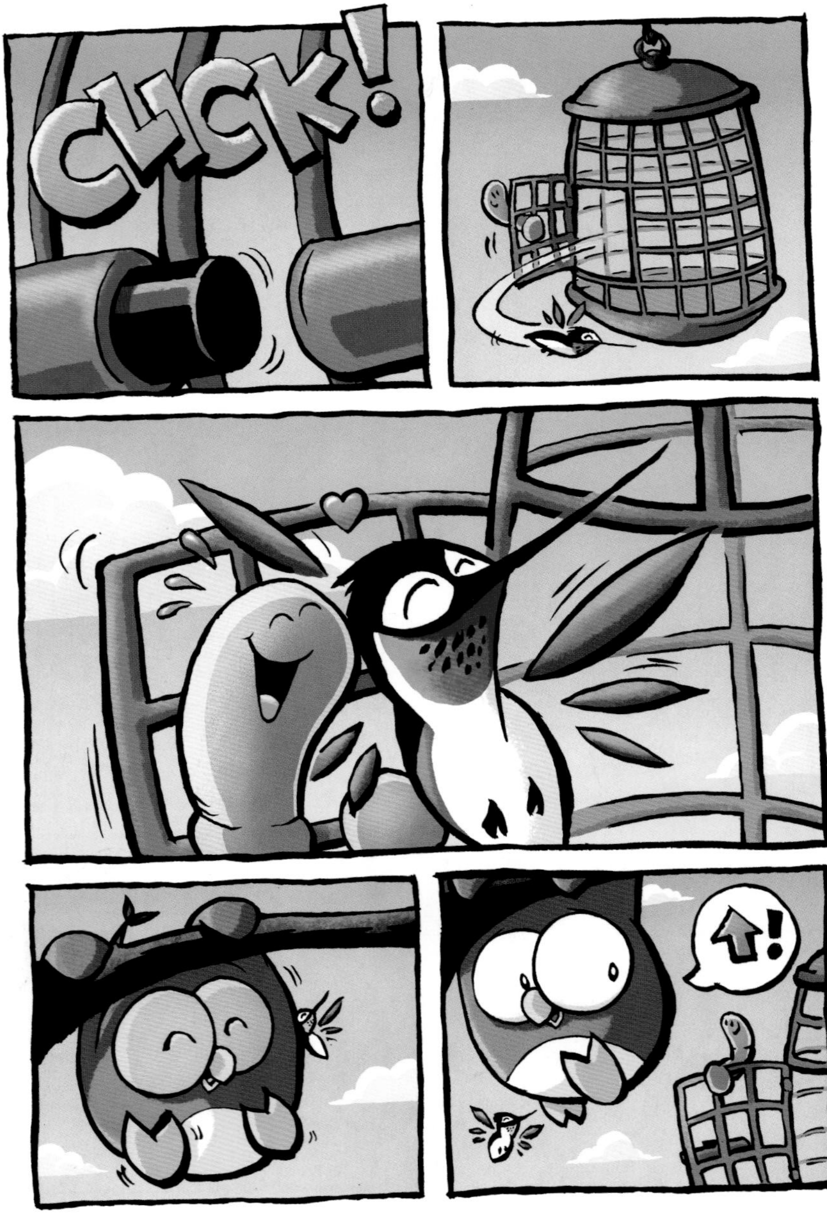
CLICK!
!

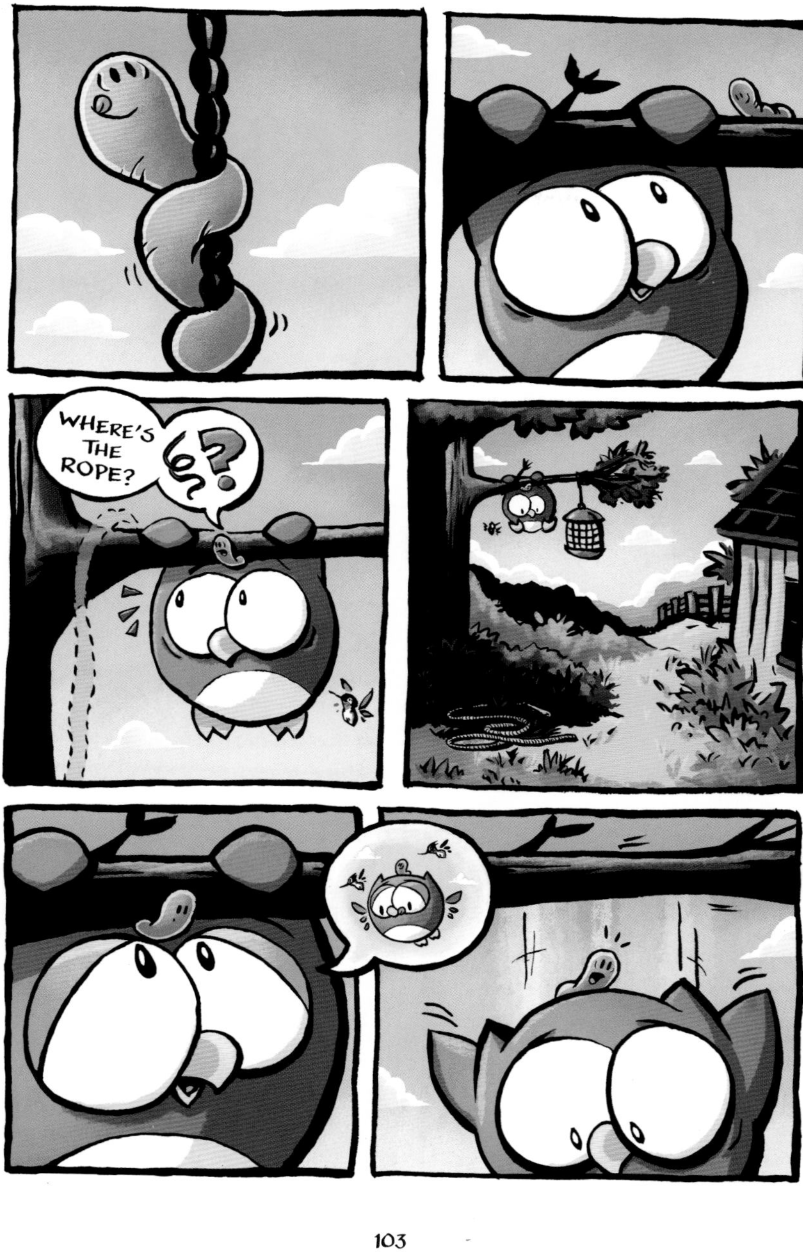
WHERE'S THE ROPE?

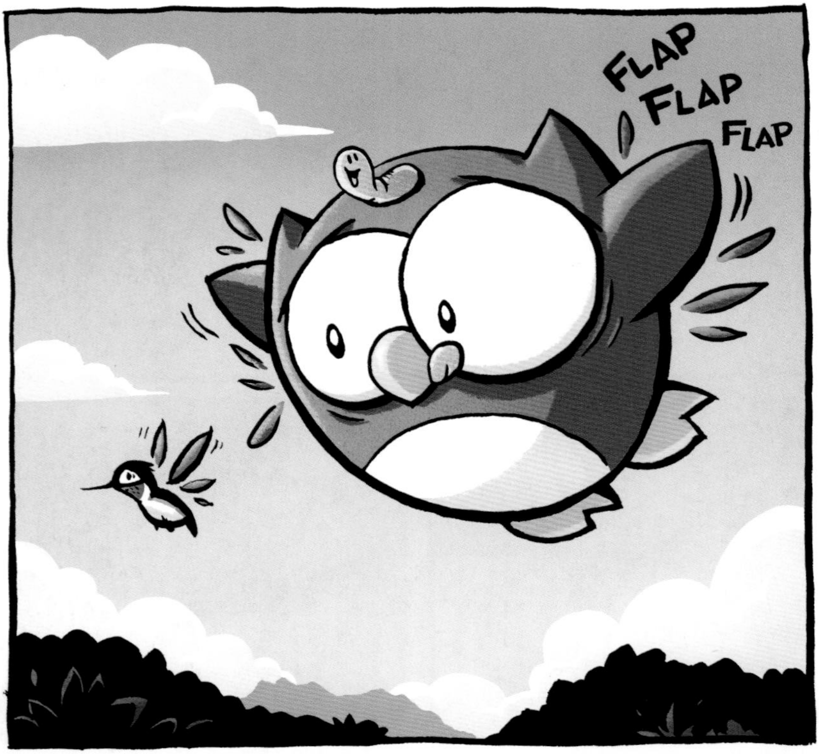
FLAP
FLAP
FLAP

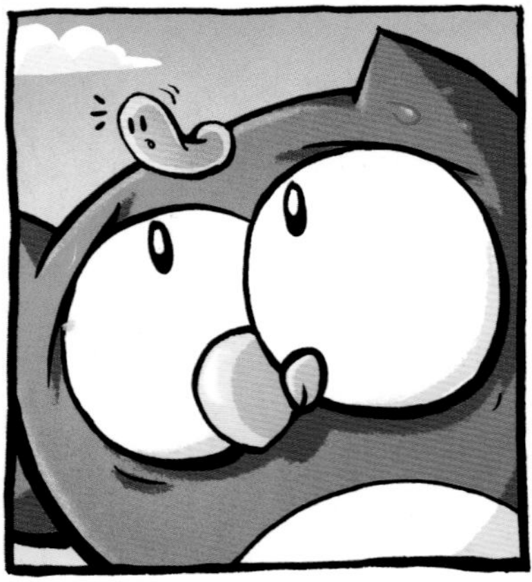

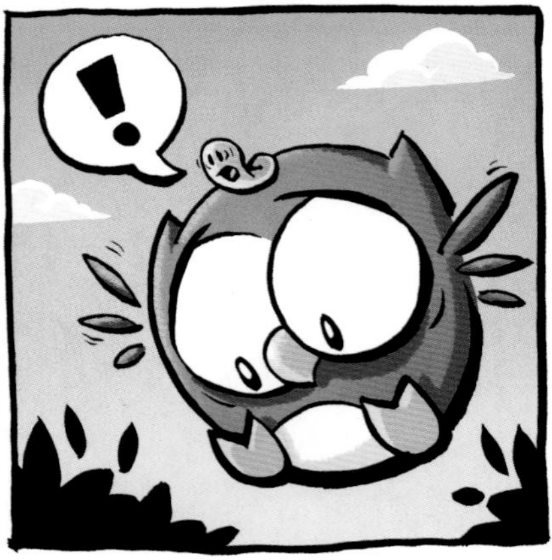
!

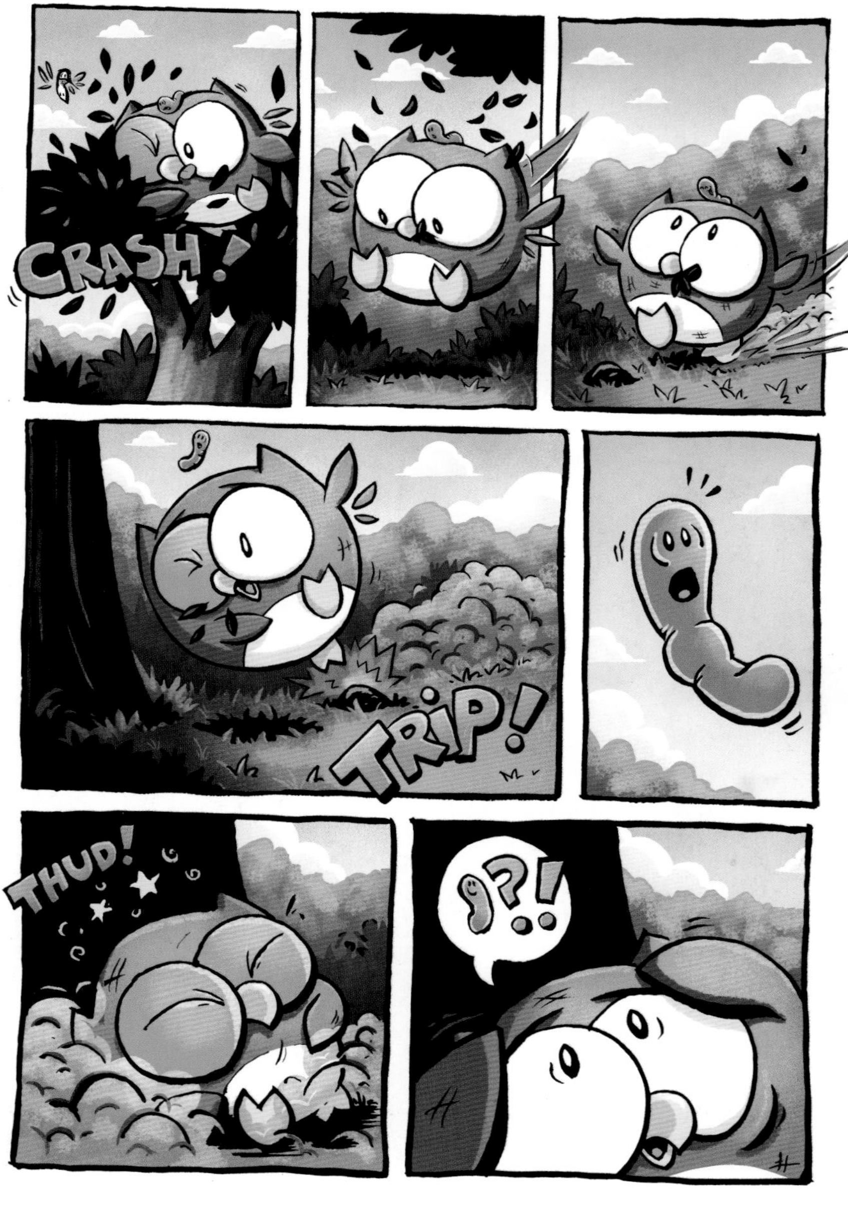
CRASH!
TRIP!
THUD!
?!

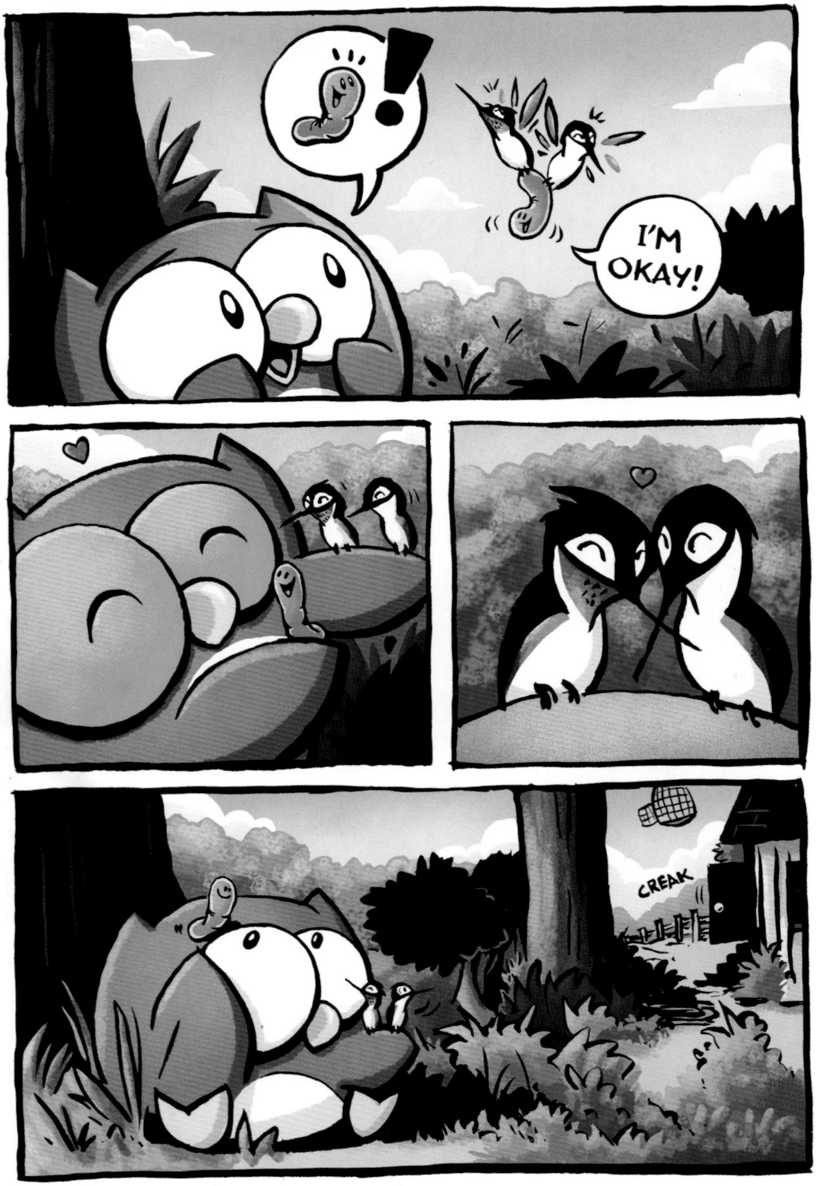
!
I'M OKAY!
CREAK

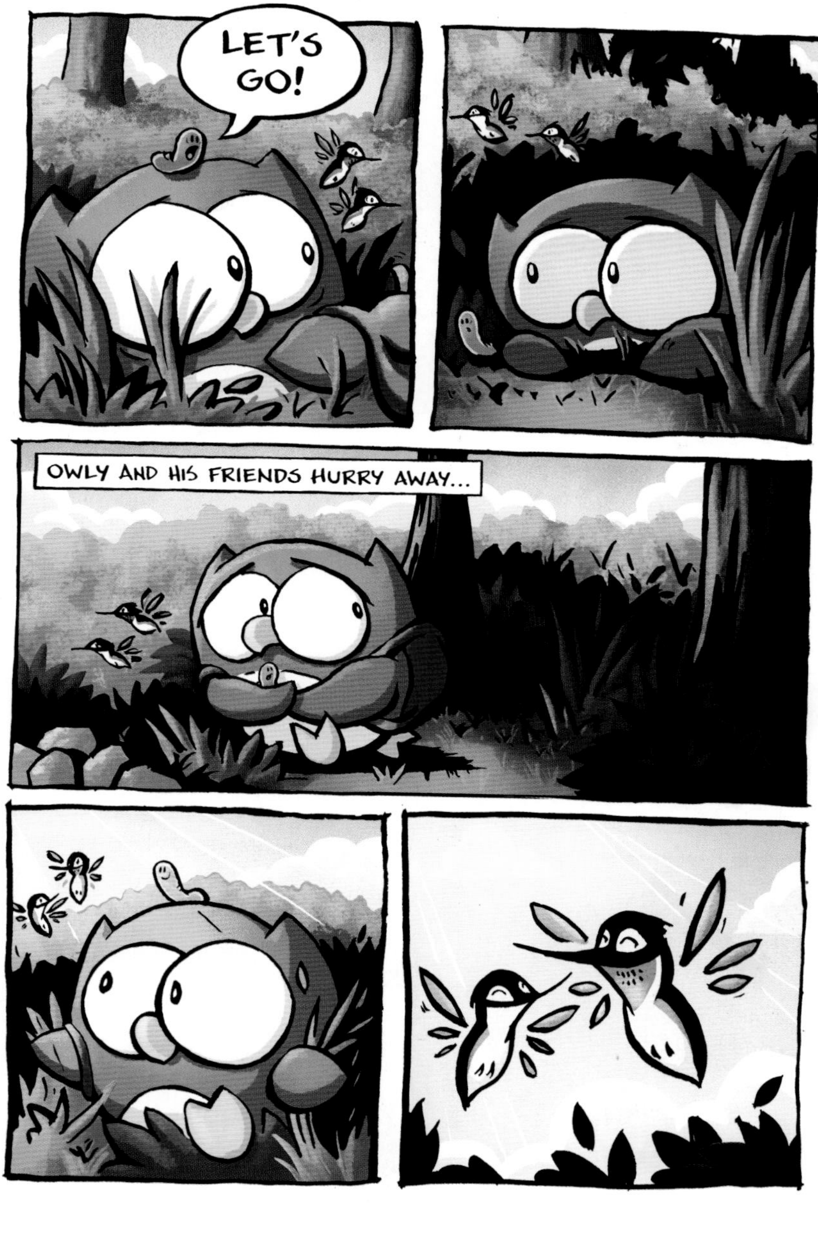
LET'S GO!
OWLY AND HIS FRIENDS HURRY AWAY...

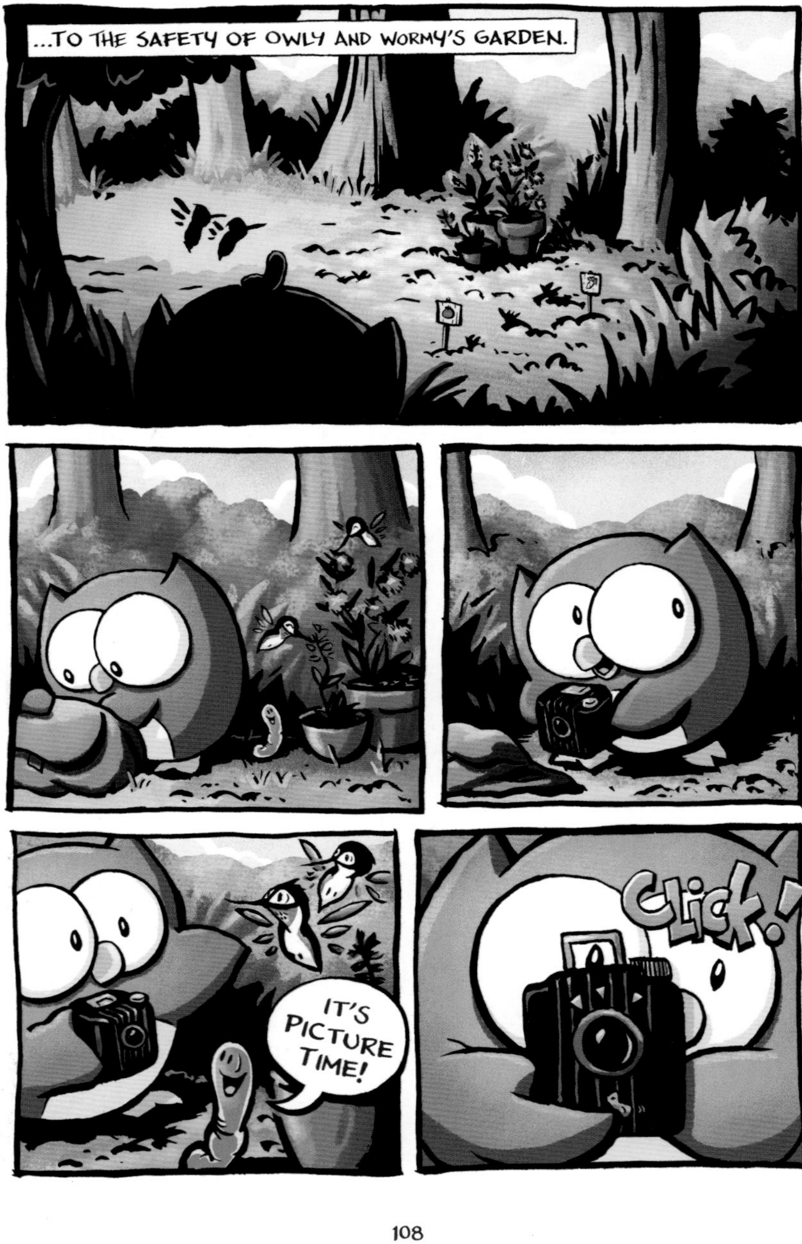
...TO THE SAFETY OF OWLY AND WORMY'S GARDEN.
IT'S PICTURE TIME!
CLICK!

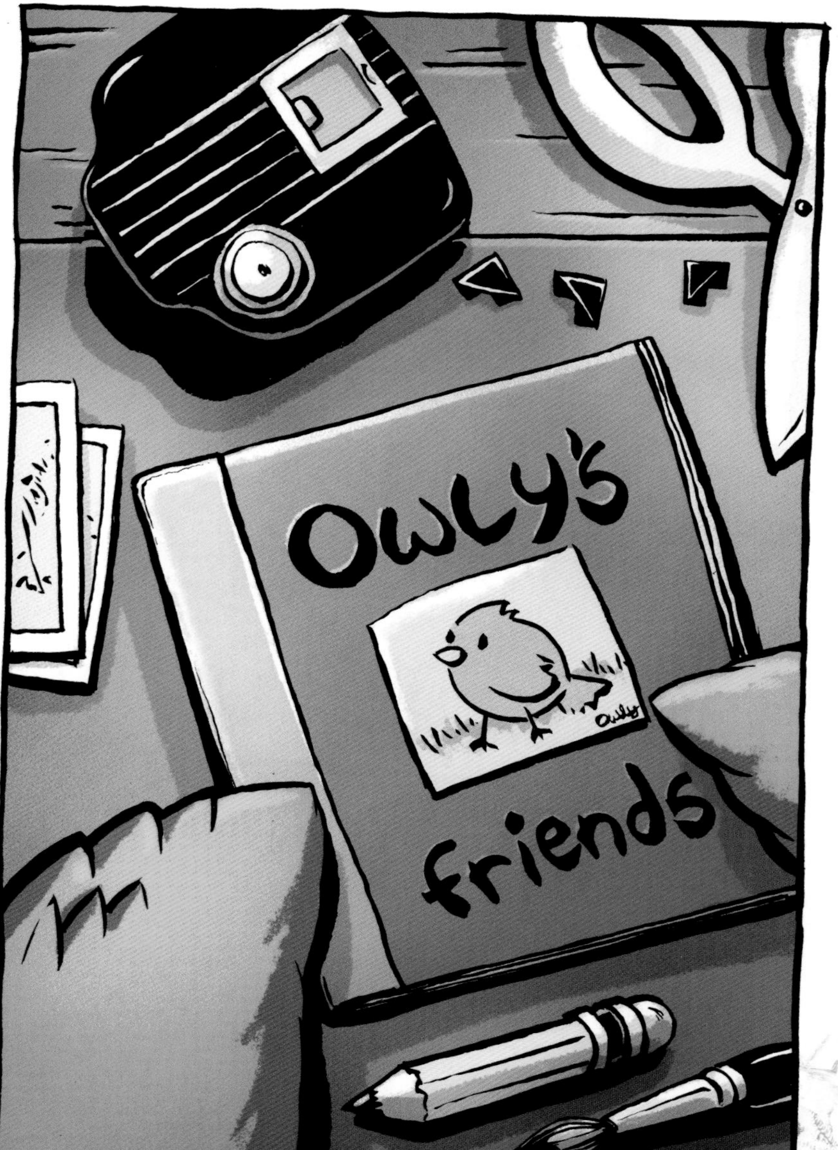
Owly's
friends
Owly

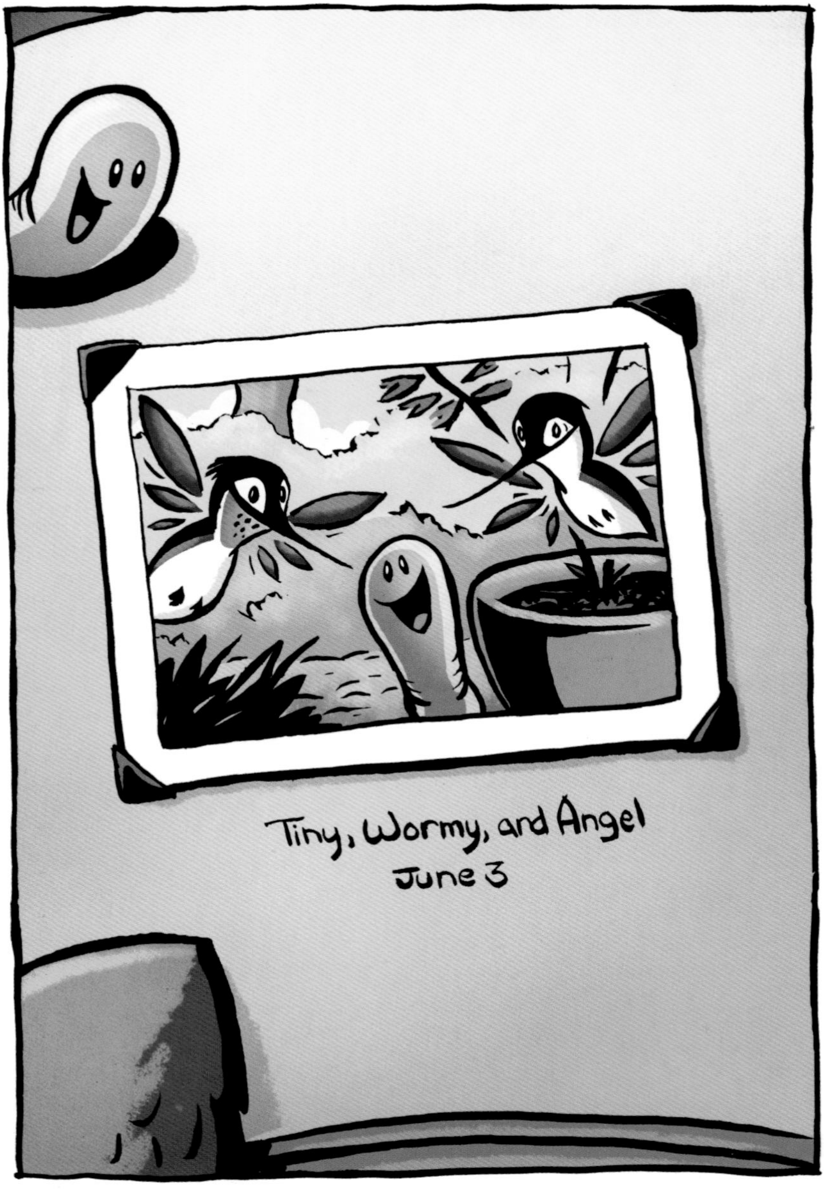
Tiny, Wormy, and Angel
June 3

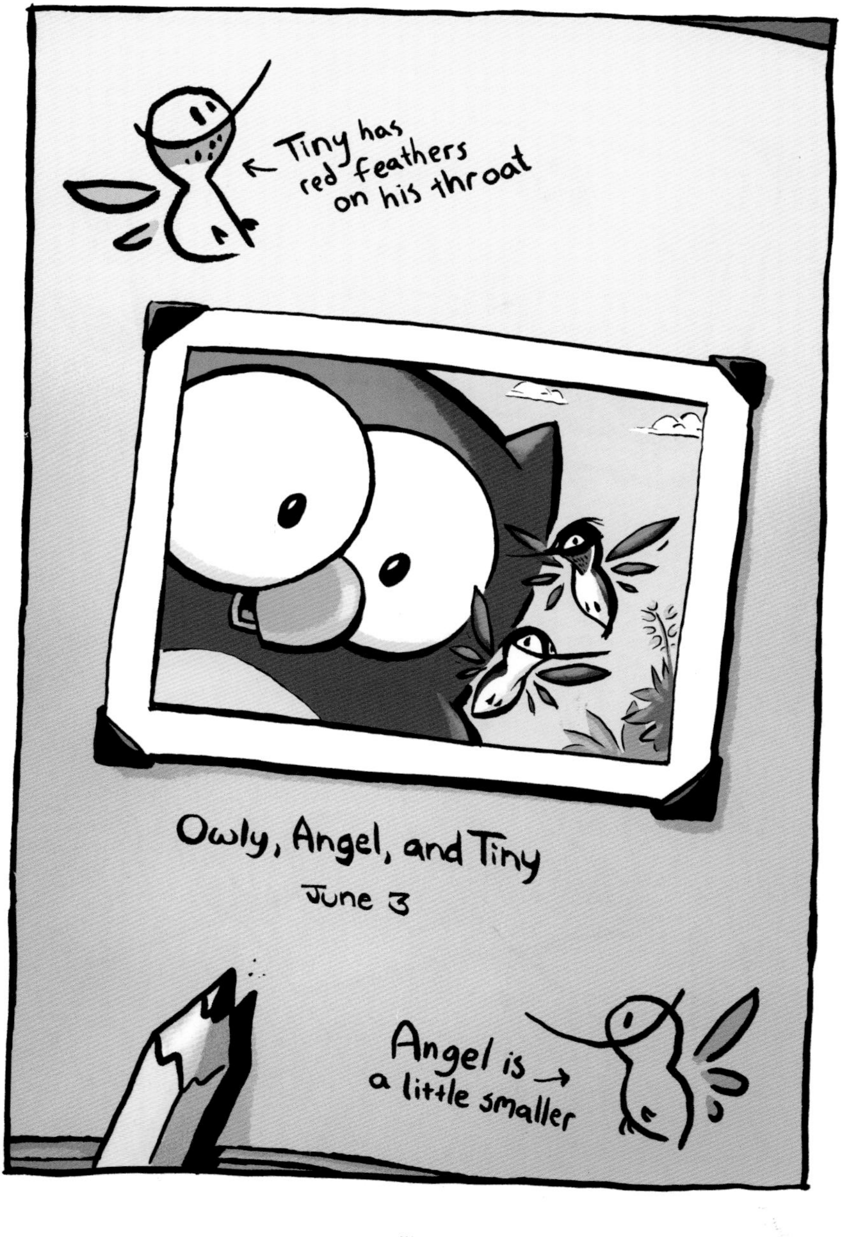
Tiny has
red feathers
on his throat
Owly, Angel, and Tiny
June 3
Angel is
a little smaller

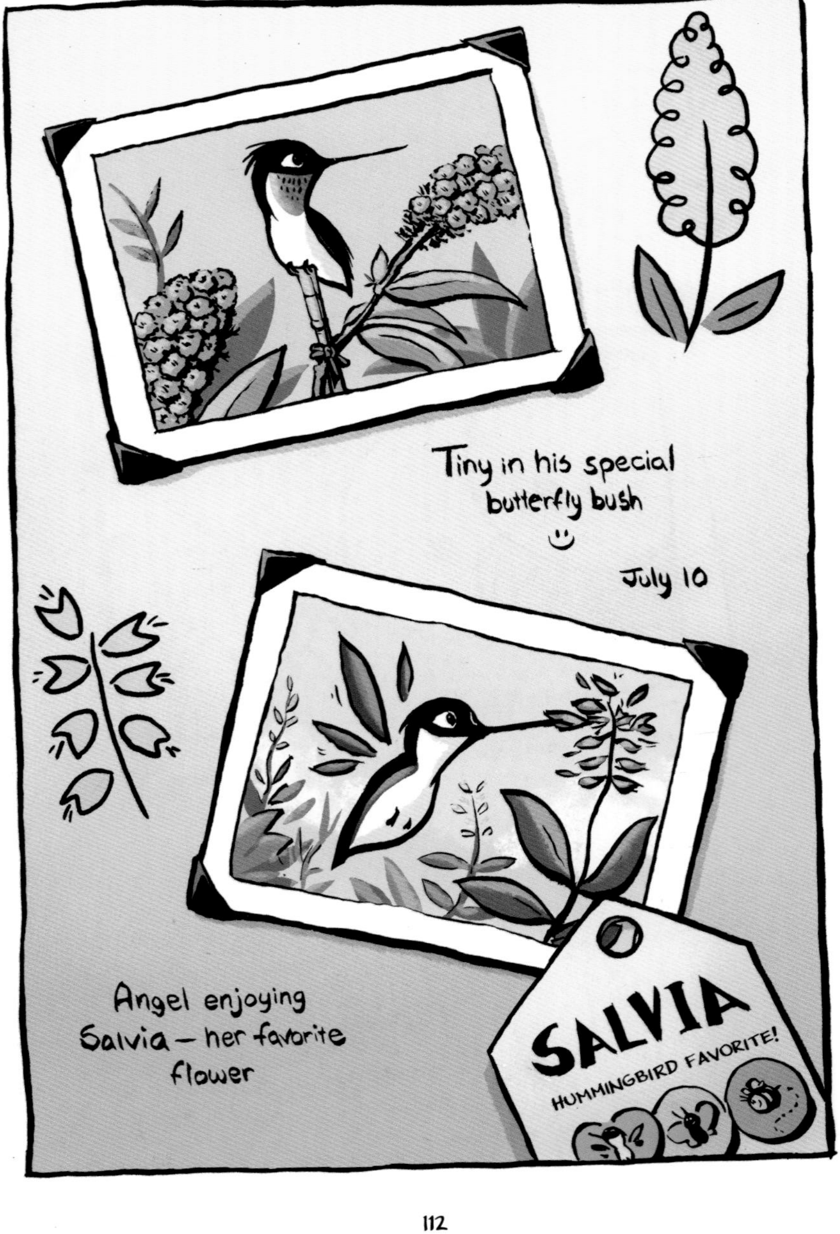
Tiny in his special
butterfly bush
July 10
Angel enjoying
Salvia — her favorite
flower
SALVIA
HUMMINGBIRD FAVORITE!

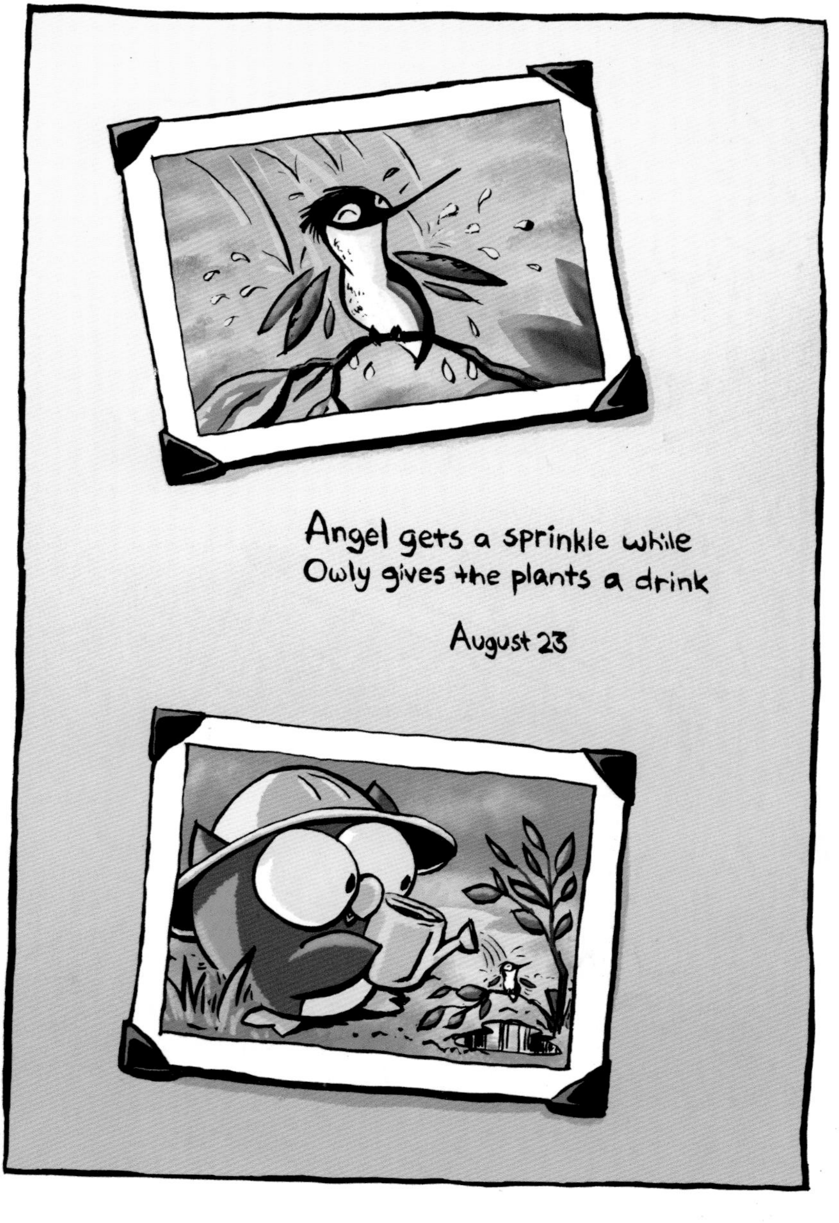
Angel gets a sprinkle while
Owly gives the plants a drink
August 23

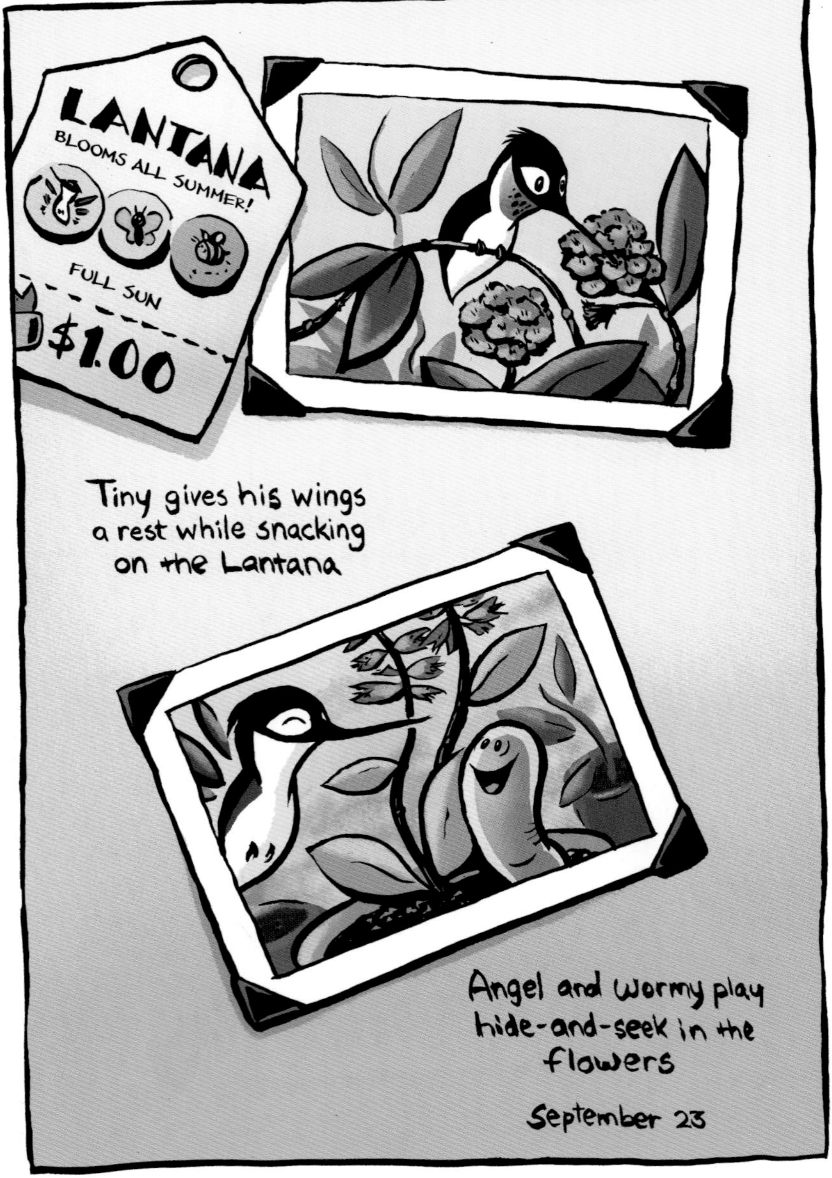
LANTANA
BLOOMS ALL SUMMER!
FULL SUN
$1.00
Tiny gives his wings a rest while snacking on the Lantana
Angel and wormy play hide-and-seek in the flowers
September 23

Owly and Wormy in
the hummingbird garden.
It's getting a little chilly.
Fall is here!

Owly and Wormy's friends
always make them happy

October 5

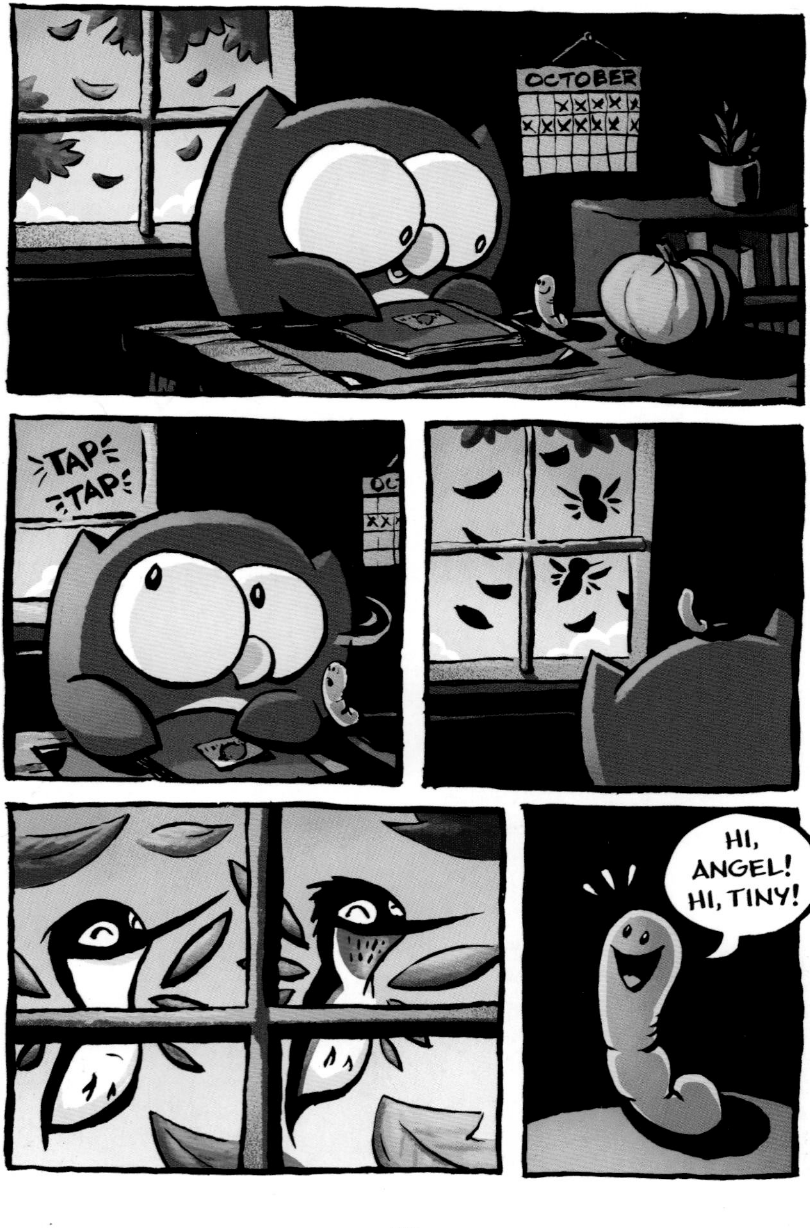
OCTOBER
TAP
TAP
HI, ANGEL! HI, TINY!

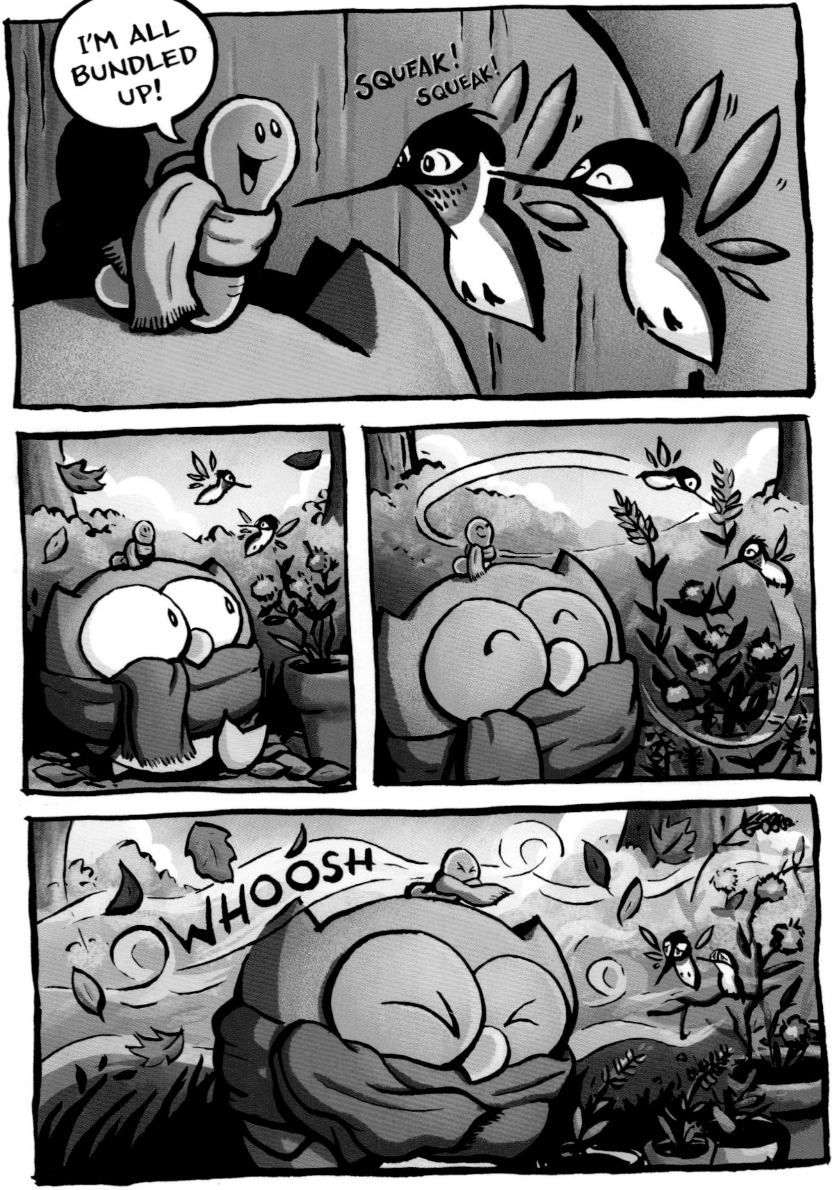
I'M ALL BUNDLED UP!
SQUEAK! SQUEAK!
WHOOSH

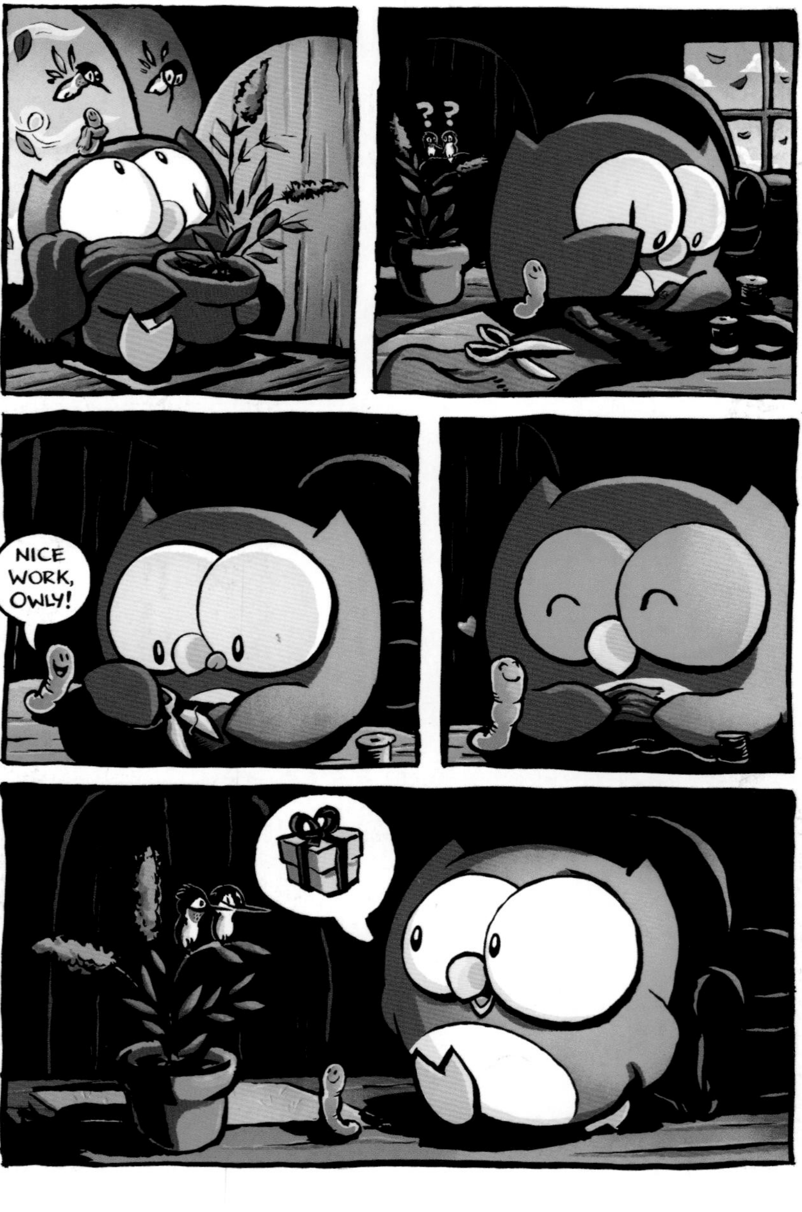
NICE WORK, OWLY!

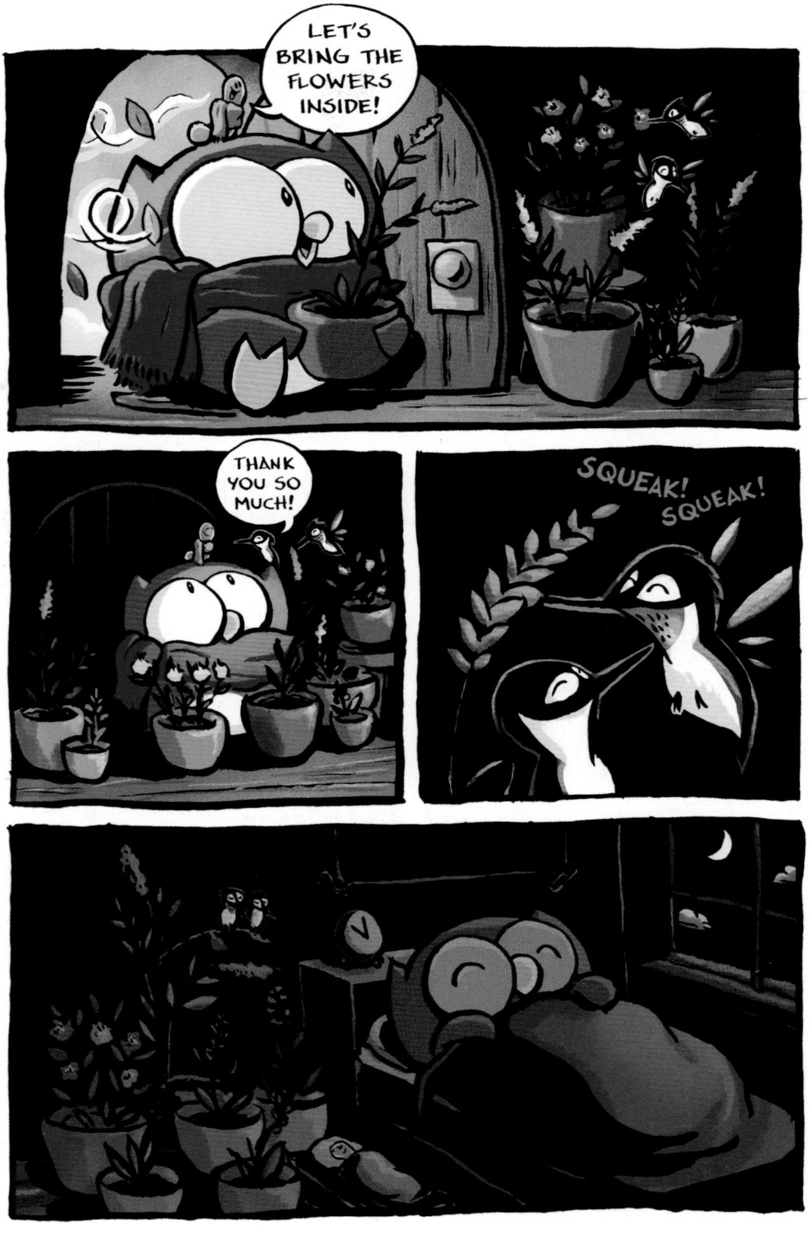
LET'S BRING THE FLOWERS INSIDE!
THANK YOU SO MUCH!
SQUEAK!
SQUEAK!

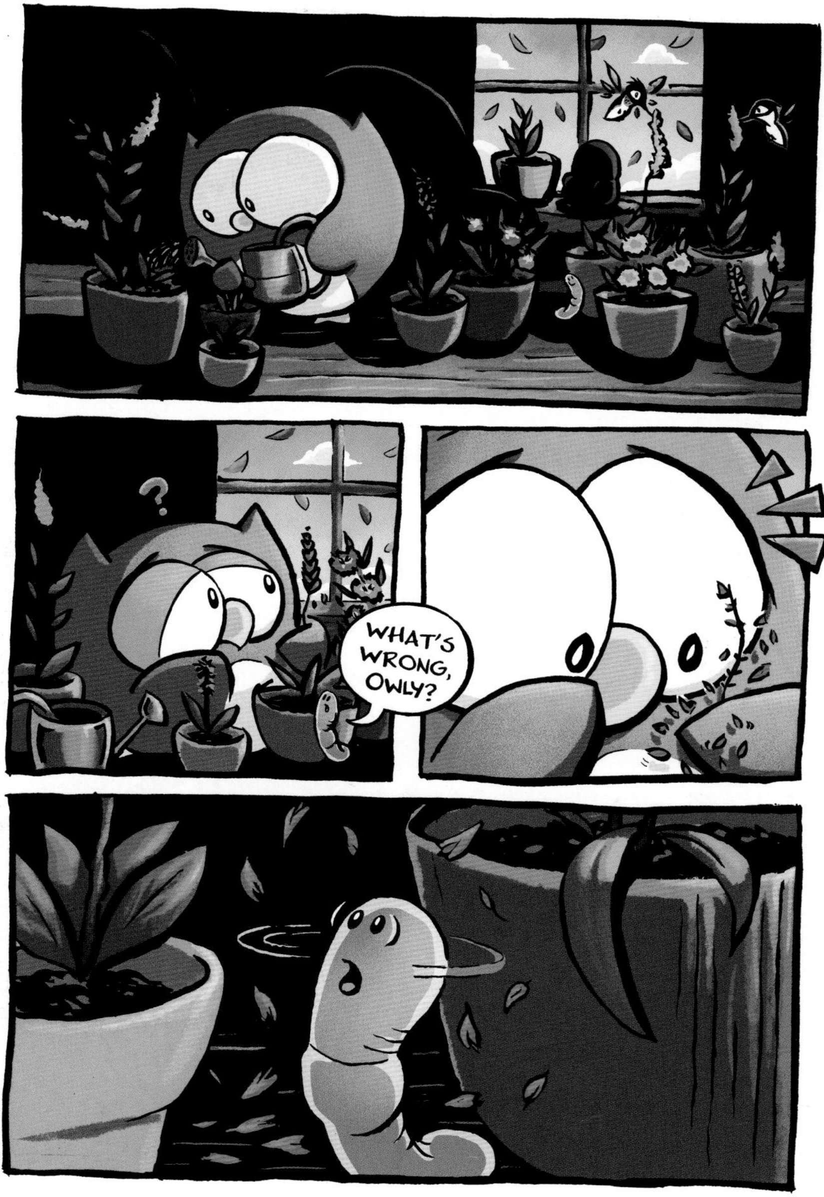
?
WHAT'S WRONG, OWLY?

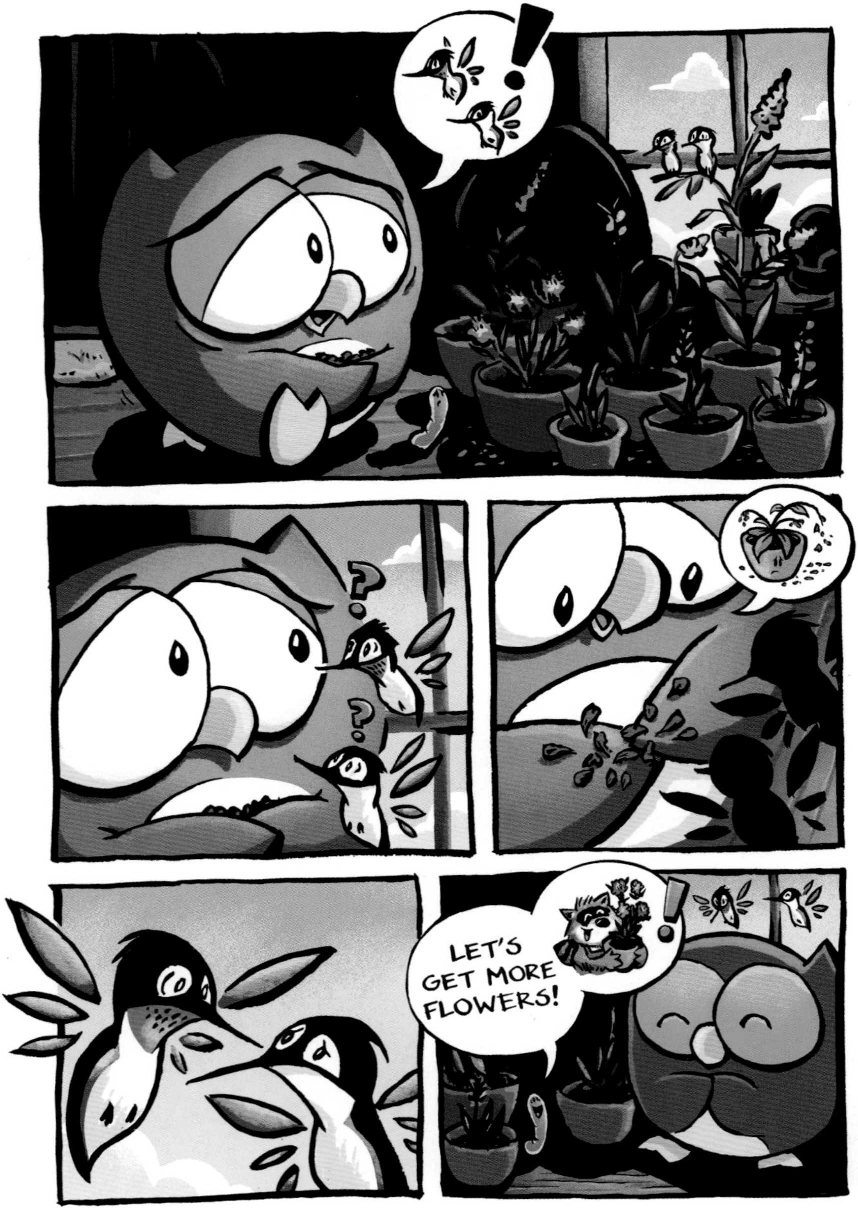
LET'S GET MORE FLOWERS!

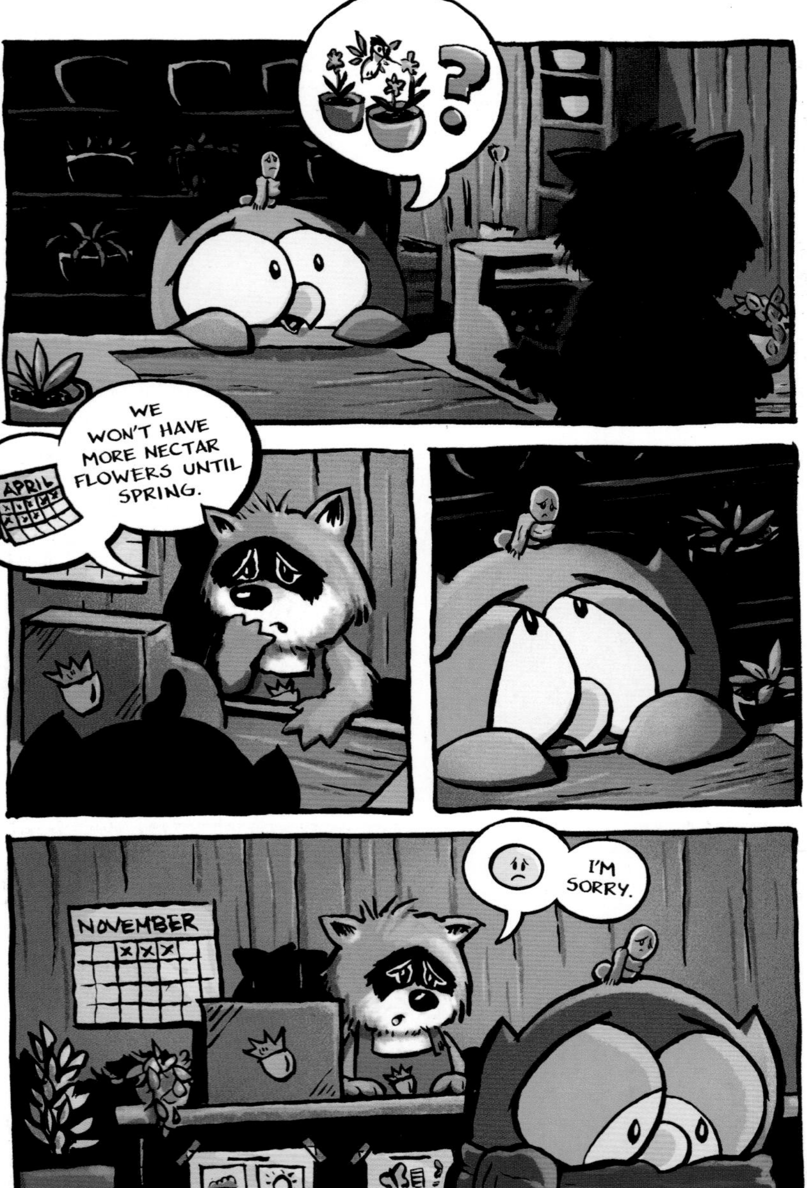

WE WON'T HAVE MORE NECTAR FLOWERS UNTIL SPRING.
APRIL
I'M SORRY.
NOVEMBER

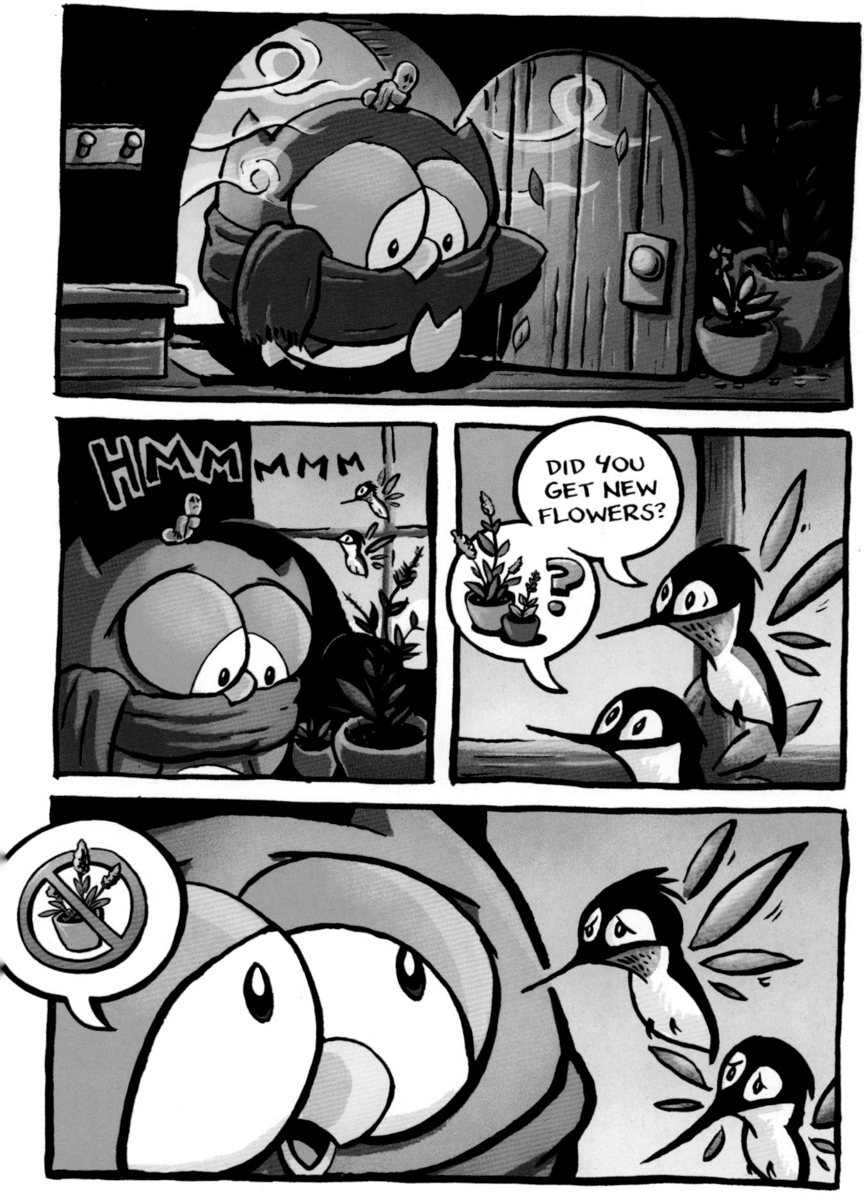
HMMMMMM
DID YOU GET NEW FLOWERS?

130

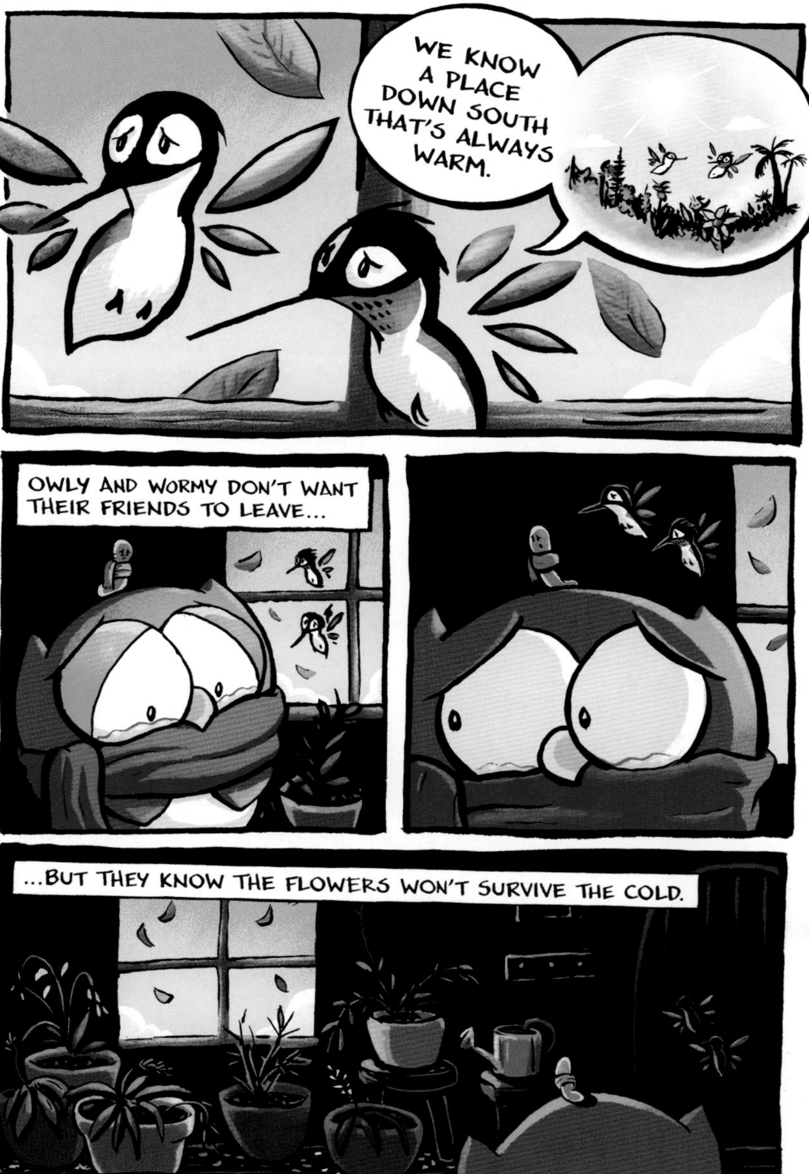
WE KNOW A PLACE DOWN SOUTH THAT'S ALWAYS WARM.
OWLY AND WORMY DON'T WANT THEIR FRIENDS TO LEAVE...
...BUT THEY KNOW THE FLOWERS WON'T SURVIVE THE COLD.

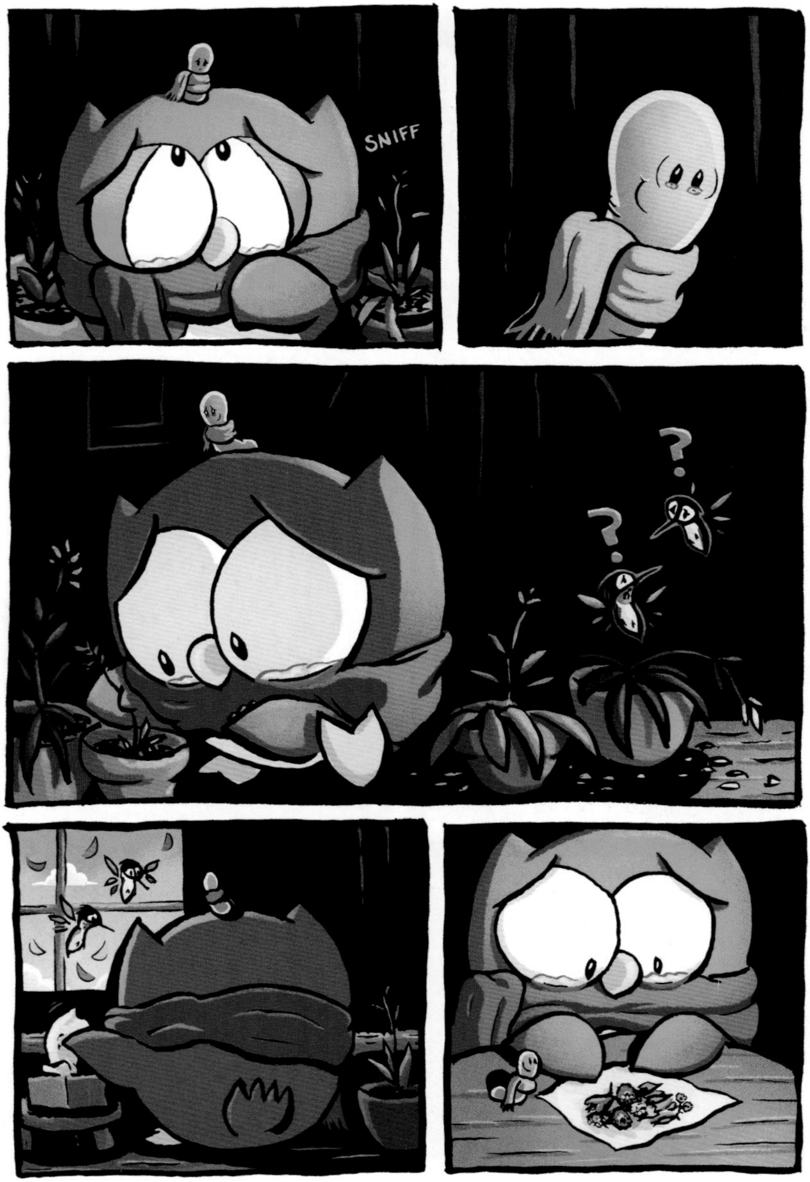
SNIFF
?
?

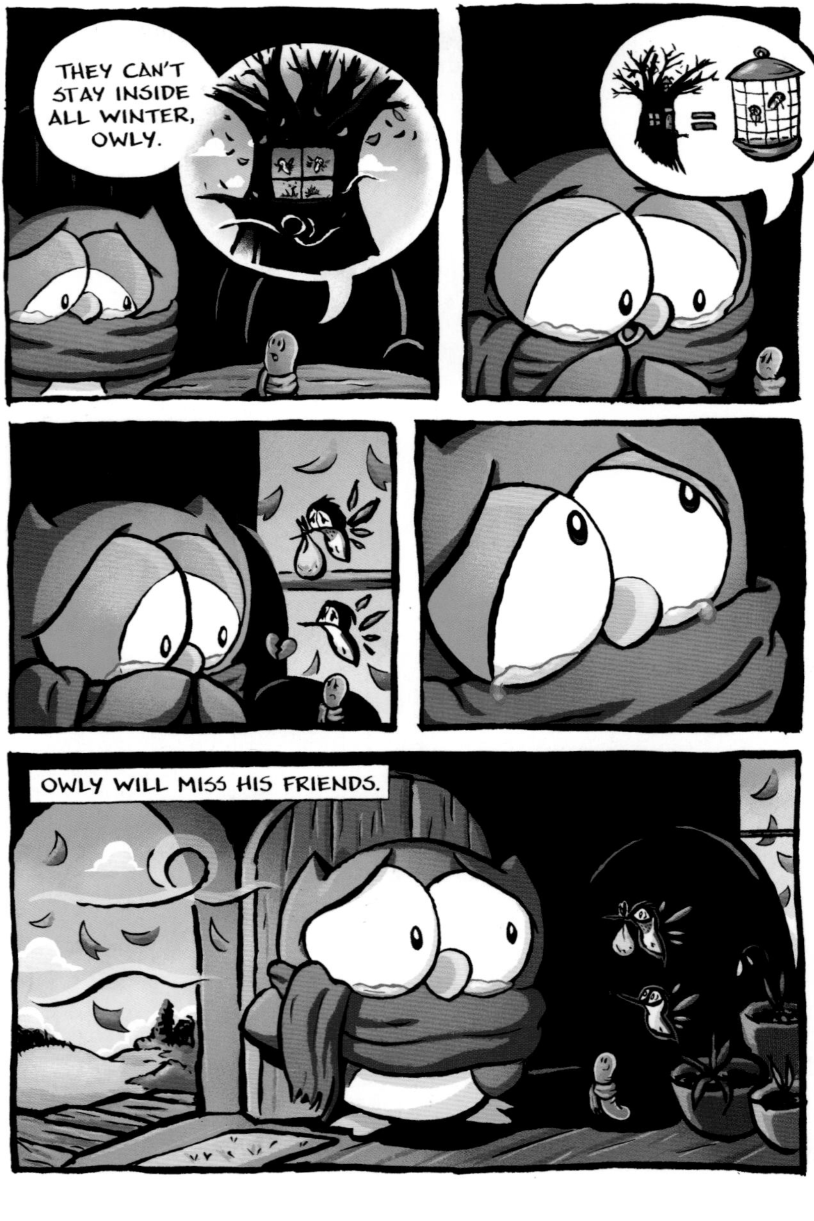
THEY CAN'T STAY INSIDE ALL WINTER, OWLY.
OWLY WILL MISS HIS FRIENDS.

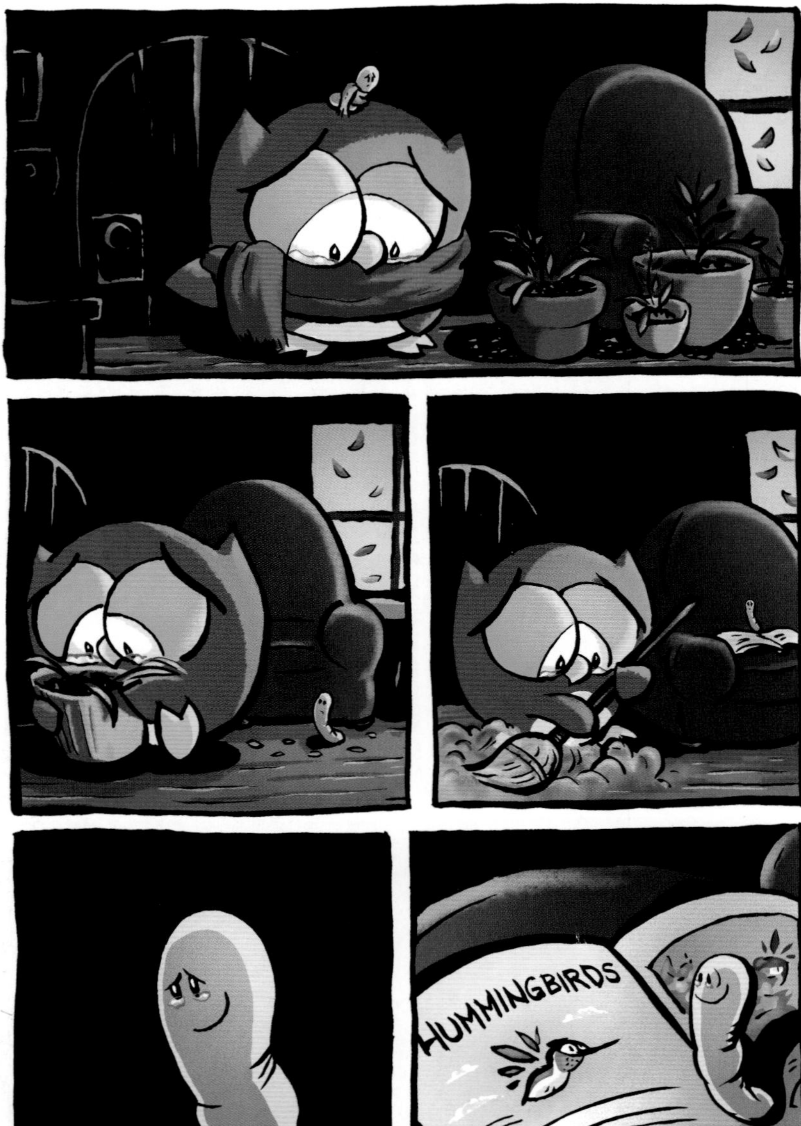
HUMMINGBIRDS

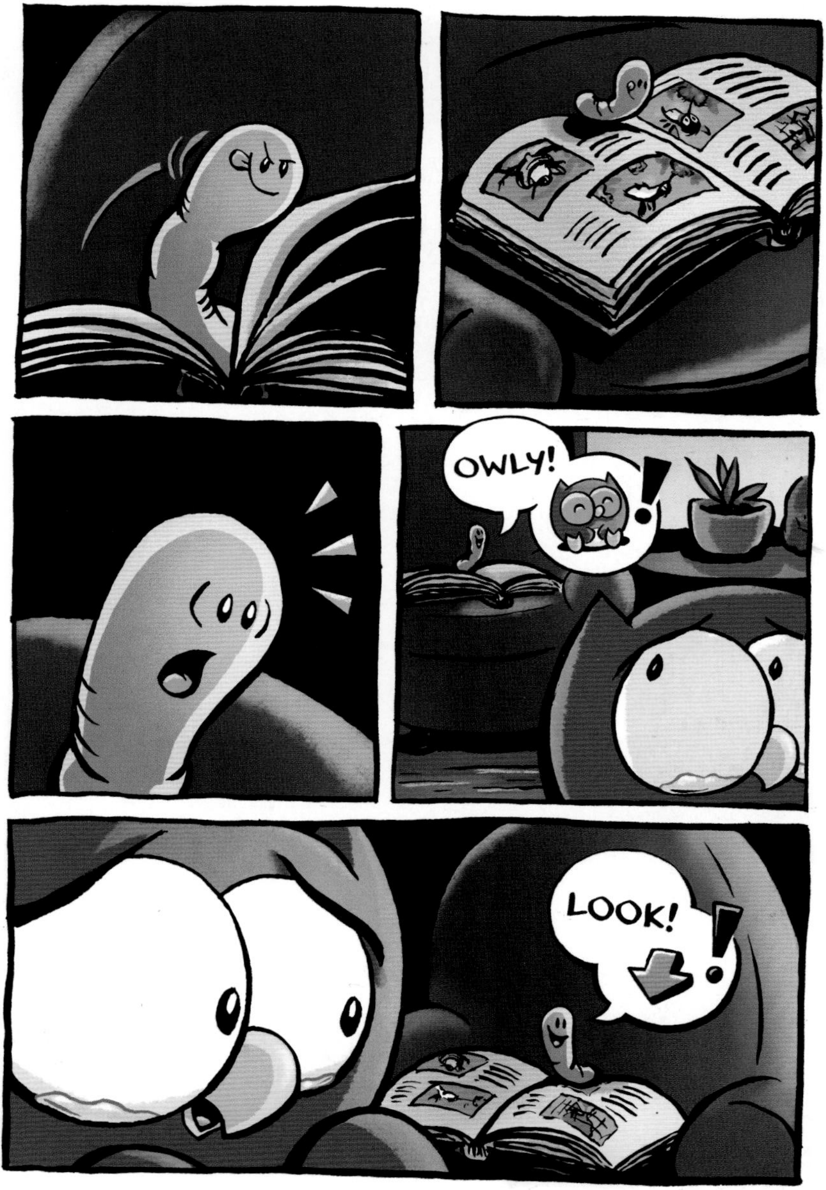
OWLY!
LOOK!

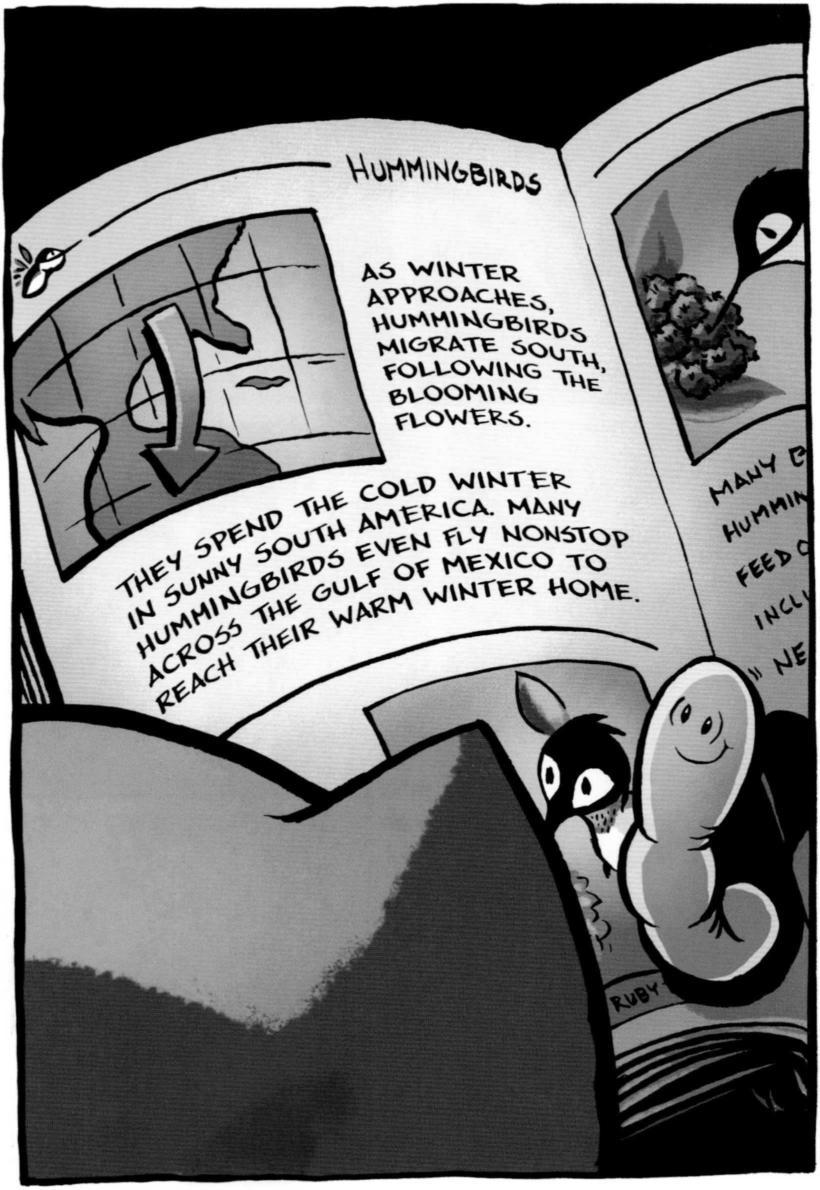
HUMMINGBIRDS
AS WINTER APPROACHES, HUMMINGBIRDS MIGRATE SOUTH, FOLLOWING THE BLOOMING FLOWERS.
THEY SPEND THE COLD WINTER IN SUNNY SOUTH AMERICA. MANY HUMMINGBIRDS EVEN FLY NONSTOP ACROSS THE GULF OF MEXICO TO REACH THEIR WARM WINTER HOME.
MANY
HUMMIN
FEED
INCL
NE
RUBY-

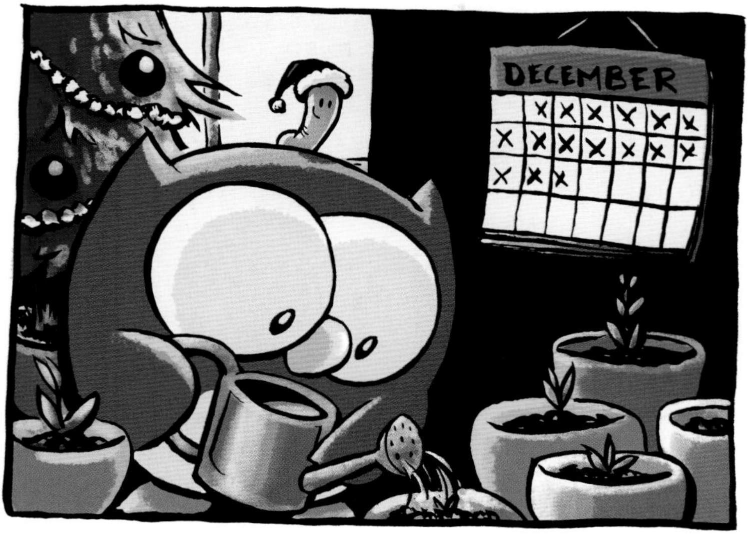
DECEMBER

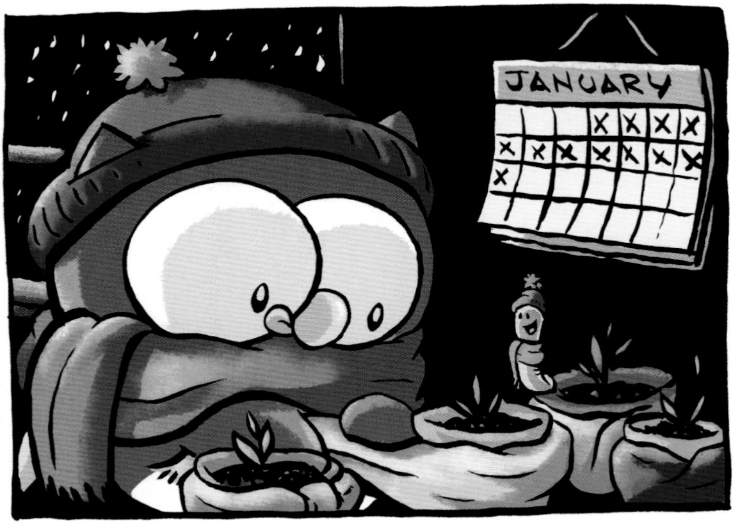
JANUARY

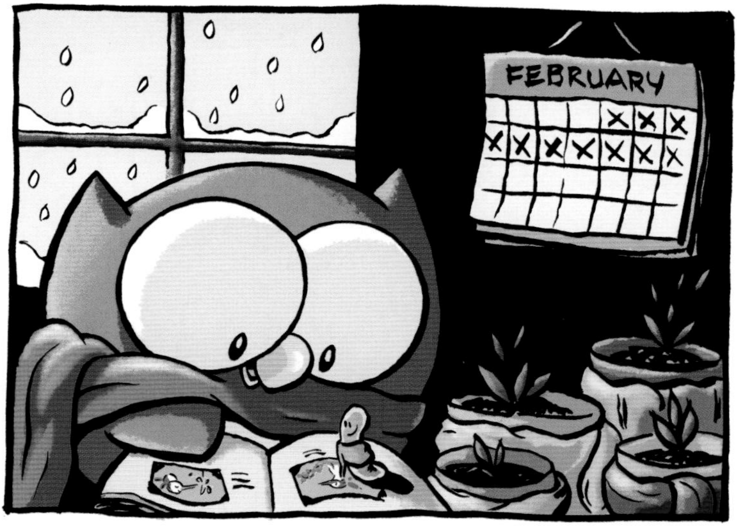
FEBRUARY

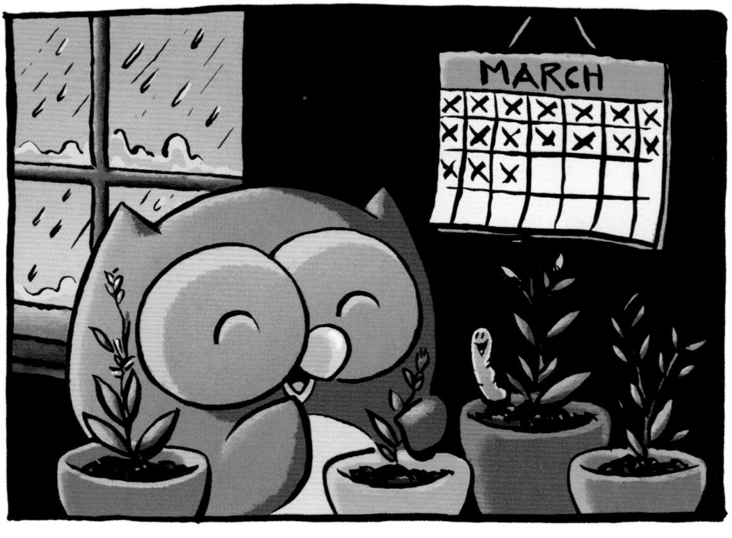
MARCH

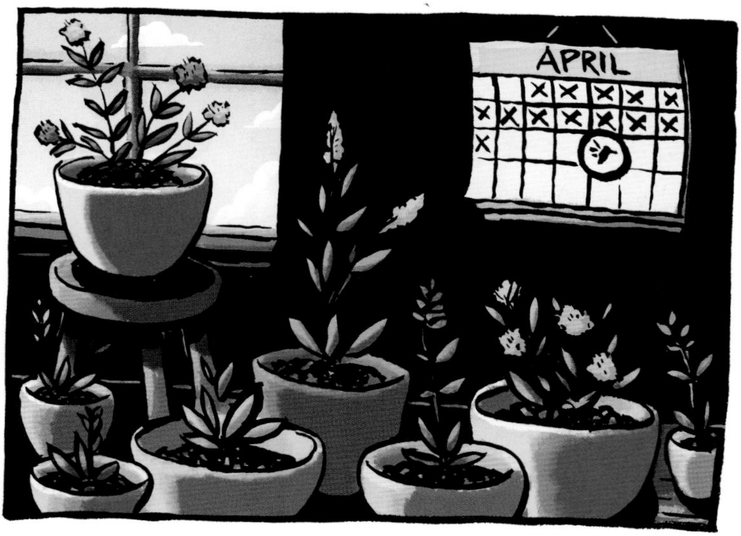
APRIL

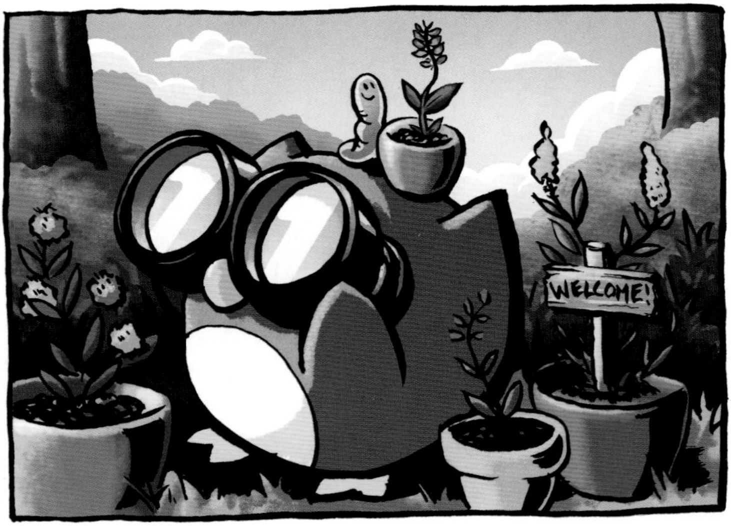
WELCOME!

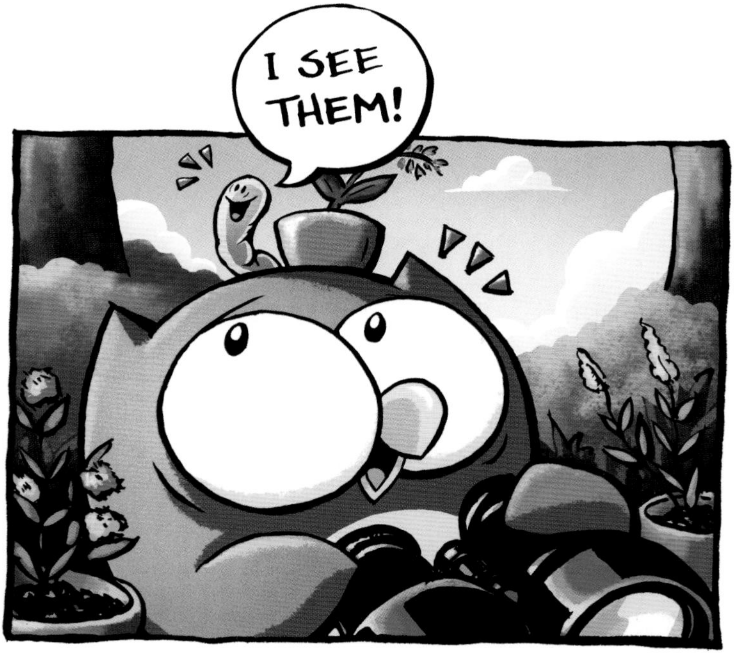
I SEE THEM!

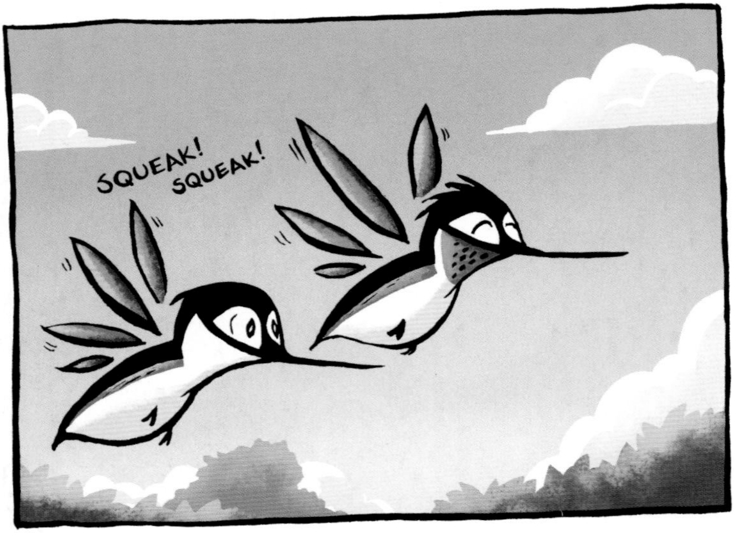
SQUEAK!
SQUEAK!

THE
END

MORE OWLY
ADVENTURES TO COME!

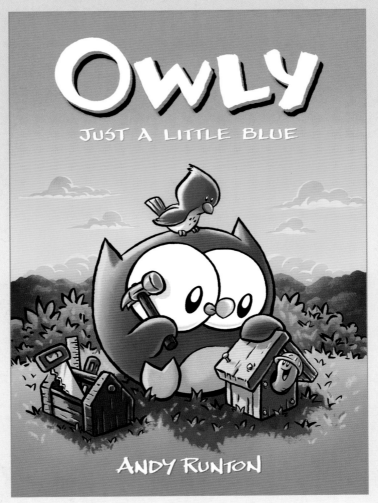

OWLY

JUST A LITTLE BLUE

ANDY RUNTON

SPECIAL THANKS
TO ALL THE OWLY FANS
AND TO MY FAMILY AND FRIENDS
FOR THEIR INCREDIBLE SUPPORT! ʚ

ESPECIALLY TO RAINA FOR BELIEVING IN ME,
TO ANA & JILL FOR THEIR GUIDANCE,
TO BARRY FOR CHAMPIONING OWLY,
TO DAVID FOR NEVER GIVING UP,
AND TO MEGAN, PHIL, AND EVERYONE AT
SCHOLASTIC GRAPHIX FOR ALL OF THEIR
HARD WORK, GUIDANCE, AND FOR
WELCOMING OWLY INTO THE FAMILY.

COLORING ASSISTANCE PROVIDED BY
WES DZIOBA & PATTY RUNTON.
I COULDN'T HAVE DONE IT
WITHOUT THEIR HELP.
THANK YOU!

ANDY RUNTON

is the award-winning creator of Owly, which has earned him multiple awards, including the Eisner Award for Best Publication for a Younger Audience. The Owly books have been praised for their "charm, wisdom, and warmth" by *Booklist*, and WIRED.com said they are "one of the best comics for kids around. Period." Andy lives in the greater Atlanta area, where he works full time as a writer and illustrator. Visit him online at andyrunton.com.

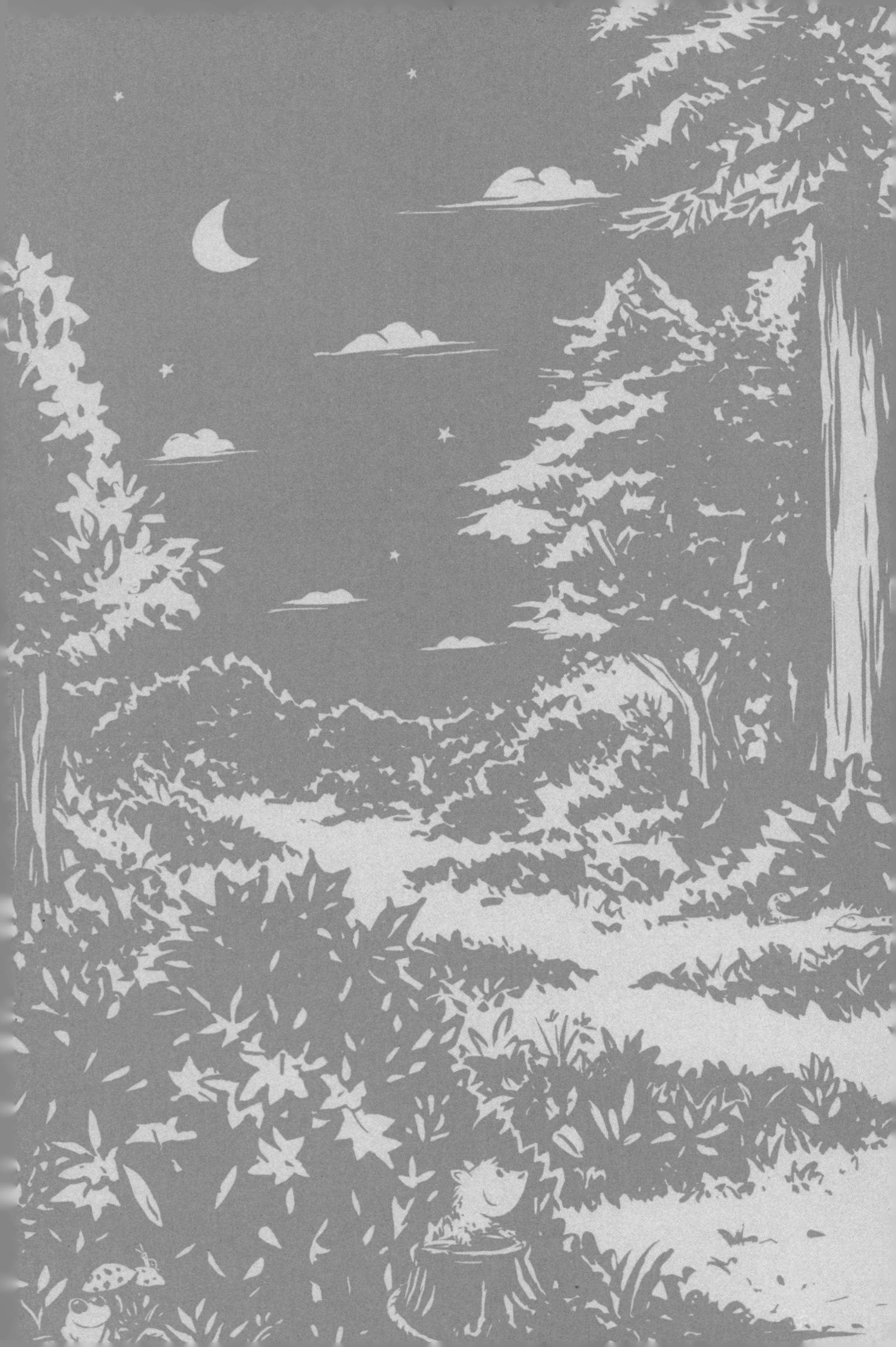